LOST HEART

When the First World War ends, Annie Fletcher waits in vain for her sweetheart, Tom, to return. In the meantime, she throws herself into Tom's dream of running his own business by opening a grocery shop. In a large house nearby live Lord and Lady Hetherington and their sons, George and Edward, known as Ted. Ted is in love with Annie, but he knows her heart belongs to Tom. But when Ted goes to work in France, he makes an unexpected discovery which is to change Annie's life forever . . .

JOYCE JOHNSON

LOST HEART

Complete and Unabridged

LINFORD
Leicester

First published in Great Britain in 2000

First Linford Edition
published 2003

British Library CIP Data

Johnson, Joyce, *1931* –
    Lost heart.—Large print ed.—
Linford romance library
    1. Love stories
    2. Large type books
    I. Title
    813.5′4 [F]

    ISBN 0–7089–4980–0

Published by
F. A. Thorpe (Publishing)
Anstey, Leicestershire

Set by Words & Graphics Ltd.
Anstey, Leicestershire
Printed and bound in Great Britain by
T. J. International Ltd., Padstow, Cornwall

This book is printed on acid-free paper

1

Annie Fletcher lay in her bed and willed morning light to come swiftly. She'd hardly slept all night, excitement chasing vivid dreams through her brain, dreams of Tom. She slid her arm from under the eiderdown's warmth and leaned out of bed to hold aside the curtain.

The edges of the window were frosted but she could just make out the pale wintry stars of the northern sky. Was he watching those same stars, thinking of her, wondering as Annie did now what the future held for them?

For a while she lay and thought of Tom, but she was awake now and it was impossible to lie idly waiting for the hours to pass. Besides there was much to do. Carefully, so as not to wake her sister, Meg, Annie slithered out of bed, stifling a gasp as her feet hit the icy linoleum. The air in the small bedroom was freezing.

She felt for her wrap and slippers, bundled them against her chest and crept out of the bedroom. She didn't want Meg to wake up yet. There'd be enough hustle and bustle all too soon, and it'd be good to have a pre-dawn hour to herself.

Privacy was a rarity in the cramped two-up, two-down, terraced house her father, Jim, was so reluctant to leave. He loved the house, he'd been born there, the youngest of ten brothers and sisters. He was the one who'd stayed in Nightingale Street, taken his bride, Joan, there and brought up his own family of three children there. He could see no reason for leaving. He would not feel comfortable anywhere else.

Annie didn't mind, she was about to fly the nest, for Tom had dreams, too, practical dreams he'd written about to Annie all through the dreadful years of the First World War. Today marked the end of those years. Today Tom was coming home, back to Yorkshire and his home town of Castlethorpe. Annie shivered with anticipation rather than the cold as she groped her way downstairs. No sound from Mam and Dad's room, but she didn't light the gas until she was safely down in the back kitchen. The mantel clock showed quarter to five.

She raked the embers in the grate, still warm from the night before, added sticks and coal and soon firelight shadows were dancing round the room. Water in the big kettle on the trivet would take a while to heat so in the meantime she set out jugs, soap and towels, and fetched the tin bath from the scullery. In the larder she could see the evidence of their advance preparation for the celebration do — fruit cakes, pies, boiled hams and sausages side by side in the cool larder, waiting to be devoured by hordes of hungry Fletchers.

The growing heat in the kitchen

softened the sharp grip of winter weather outside. She stretched and yawned, luxuriating in the warmth and unaccustomed silence in the house. When the water was ready she kneeled in the tin bath and with economical movements born of long practice washed herself all over and soaped her hair. It was a darker blonde than her sister's and Tom'd liked the way she wore it, caught in a ribbon at the back. But she'd been sixteen then. Maybe now it'd be better in the newer fashionable bob. After today she'd decide.

Nearly six o'clock. Annie dried herself, put on an old frock over her new underwear and sat cross-legged before the fire, her thick hair a damp curtain in front of her face. As it began to dry it curled and waved under the regular brush strokes, rhythmic, soothing.

Will he? Won't he? Brushstroke.

Do I? Don't I? Brushstroke.

It was a game she often played.

Does he love me? A long, downward stroke.

Do I love him? The brush stopped midway and dropped in her lap. She shut her eyes and saw Tom's face as clearly as the last time she'd seen him on his last leave two years earlier. Then she was sixteen, Tom twenty, a confident young man already blistered by nearly two years' war in France, but his smile had said it all. He'd be back. Tom Ormeroyd had told her he was a survivor. His final kiss had promised much more for the future and the small silver ring he'd slipped on her finger had sealed that promise. His words still rang in her head as clearly now as then.

'We'll be married just as soon as possible after I'm back, Annie. There's no stopping that. We're made for each other, you and I, whatever happens. Never forget that.'

She'd clung to him then, tears welling in her dark eyes, desperation in her arms as she held on to him. Gently he'd disengaged himself, touched her cheek with his finger, smiled, and left, along with Vincent, her brother, who was in the same regiment as Tom.

After that just two years of letters. She flushed again, remembering. Among some of the more recent letters one said passionate and wonderfully loving things, practical as well, mapping out their future together. Tom was a man of vision. The narrow streets of Castlethorpe wouldn't confine him for long if he survived the war. He was going somewhere in the world and he was taking Annie with him. All these letters were in a locked box in the deepest corner of Annie's wardrobe, letters which were her future.

A creak above stairs startled her out of her dreams. Mam and Dad were stirring and the day they'd prayed for was about to begin. It was just as well Annie had had her quiet hour for it was the last one of the day. As soon as Jim and Joan Fletcher came downstairs things really started to hum. Joan gave her orders.

'Meg, you see to the kettle, and toast those balm cakes I made yesterday. Annie, put eggs on to boil, two apiece, and I'll make the porridge. We won't be having any dinner midday so we'll need a good breakfast. Look sharp now. Time'll fly till train time.'

After breakfast came an orgy of bread-making, more pies, trifles to finish off, and great piles of sandwiches to cut, enough to feed the entire British army for a month it seemed and still Joan worried they hadn't done enough.

'Bess and Albert'll be fetching more stuff, too,' Jim remonstrated. 'You mustn't put their noses out of joint. They'll be that glad to have Tom home at last.'

'Of course. I wouldn't dream of spoiling their moment, but our Annie and Tom, well they are promised.'

She looked meaningfully at her daughter.

'Mam, there's nothing official, and it's been two years since I . . . we've seen each other. It's a long time and he might've . . . er . . . he might not . . . '

'Don't talk rubbish. Anyone can see you're daft about each other, and that's not likely to change,' Jim said through a mouthful of nails, punctuating every word with a hammer blow to a banner above the door.

He stepped down from the chair and looked at his handiwork.

'**Welcome Home Vincent and Tom**. That do you?'

'It's champion.'

Joan was bursting with happiness. Vincent, their only son, had survived the terrible war, survived against all the odds, survived on prayer and hope. The bonus was Tom, too, Annie's young man coming home to claim his girl at last. They'd been so lucky. Not many families in Nightingale Street had come through the terror unscathed and Joan hoped their own celebrations would not be taken amiss. But she just couldn't help it, and a wedding in prospect as well. Today she felt maybe the four long waiting years might've been worth it after all.

'Of course, Tom'll think just the same of you as he did two years ago,' she echoed her husband. 'My goodness, you've written enough letters between you to paper the parlour. Mind, you shouldn't rush into anything. Plenty of time, and you're only eighteen.'

'You were seventeen when you married Dad,' young Meg piped up. 'I think it'll be lovely. Will you have a house of your own, Annie?'

'I don't know. I wish you'd not talk as though . . . as though it were all signed and sealed. Let's get the lads home first.'

'This is a day for celebration, first and foremost. Now look sharp and get ready for the station. We're meeting Bess and Albert there ten minutes before the train's due in.'

'Best put your warm waistcoat and muffler on,' his wife said. 'It'll be that cold at the station. Wind'll fair whistle through you. Go on, girls, move.'

Annie went into her parents' room where there was a looking-glass. How would Tom see her? She peered into the mirror, soft brown eyes glistening with anticipation. Would he find her changed?

Meg burst into the room.

'Annie, where's my red scarf? My, you look grand. Lucky Tom! If you do have a house can I come and visit? You'll have to get a place. It'd be too cramped here with Tom as well, or maybe you'll live with Aunt Bess and Uncle Albert. Their house is big enough for anything.'

'Stop, stop,' Annie cried out, holding her ears. 'Nothing's for certain yet. Your scarf's by the bed, and it's time to go. Come on!'

Annie ran downstairs where her parents were still organising last-minute details. Jim frowned at his banner, surely a bit crooked, Joan counted the sandwiches, mentally dividing them by the number of guests expected. She looked up and met Jim's eyes.

'It's here at last, Jim. Thank God it's over.'

He took her hand, blinking away his own emotion.

'Nay, it's only a beginning, love, and now we can start to live a bit without fear. Things'll be different from now on.'

Down the line the signalman switched the points, diverting the special train from London to its first stop, Castlethorpe, near Leeds. As it passed his box he cranked the telephone handle.

'Five minutes off, just gone by. Expected time of arrival, ten minutes.'

Up the line Castlethorpe's station-master stepped out of his office and waved his arms to attract the mayor's attention. He took out his watch, pointed to it, mimed ten minutes and went back to get his bowler hat. Everything must be done right and proper on this day of all days.

The mayor nudged his lady mayoress.

'Champion turn out. Grand show for

11

our heroes' homecoming.'

As the train's triumphant hooter sounded in the distance an answering cheer went up from the crowd as they pressed dangerously close to the flimsy barrier erected by the station master to prevent welcoming friends and relatives from tumbling on to the line. All faces turned eagerly in the same direction, scanning the distance for the first sight of the train.

Joan held on tight to Jim's arm and smiled at Bess and Albert Ormeroyd, Tom's uncle and aunt, who'd brought him up as their own lad ever since his parents had died of influenza a score of years ago.

'Not long now,' Joan said. 'Soon have our lads with us.'

'Not before time,' Bess's voice choked. 'It's been that quiet in the house since our Tom left.'

'He'll liven it up now, that's for sure.'

Joan stood on tiptoe, craning her head towards the track.

'And I expect your Annie's excited.'

Bess looked fondly at her nephew's sweetheart.

'It's here, it's here!'

Meg, jumping up and down, seized her sister's hand.

The band played, and the train rounded the track's curve and joined in with screeching whistle blasts. The crowd roared as the band increased its volume. As the train snaked ponderously into the station Annie tried to look in every window, searching for Tom, but there were so many men hung around doorways shouting and waving, looking for their own families, the faces merged into a flood of cheering khaki.

The returning troops were stunned by their welcome. It was almost too much after what they'd been through. One or two even turned back towards the security of the carriage, suddenly uncertain how they'd cope with this excess of emotion waiting for them. Then, as the engine slowed to a halt the crowd excelled itself throwing up a huge cheer.

Annie clasped her hands in agony as she was pushed back into the crowd by a burly corporal who seized a woman with a young child in a bear-hug of joy and relief. Tears streamed down all three faces. Annie looked away and tried to press back to the front but the wave of bodies took her in the opposite direction from her family.

A tall fair-haired man half turned and she shouted, 'Tom, Tom,' but as he turned full face she stopped, embarrassed — he was nothing like Tom. Chaos and pandemonium surrounded her on all sides as she fought and struggled against the stream for what seemed an eternity.

The band stopped playing and Mayor Ramsden gave a short, welcome-home speech, and people started to move away, anxious to get sons, husbands, fathers back in their own homes where they belonged.

As the crowd thinned, Annie was able to push her way back towards her family and her heart leaped with love as she saw two khaki figures at the centre of a cluster of Fletchers and Ormeroyds. She couldn't wait for Tom's embrace, for him to declare his love and to give hers in return. She waved.

'I'm here,' she called, a radiant smile on her face.

One of the men turned.

'Oh, Annie, love,' he said, and instantly she knew something was dreadfully wrong.

Her brother, Vincent, held out his arms to her at the same instant that she saw the second figure wasn't Tom. It was an older man, in officer's uniform.

2

'Vincent, what's wrong? Why do you look like that, and where's Tom? Hasn't he caught the train? Will he be on another one later?'

Vincent's stricken face didn't reassure her, nor did Bess Ormeroyd's shocked look of horror. Annie turned to her mother. Joan had never shied from facing the unpleasant and clearly, whatever the rest of them knew, it was very unpleasant. The officer stepped out towards her.

'Is this Corporal Ormeroyd's fiancée? Perhaps I can . . . '

Joan put a protective arm around Annie.

'No, I'll talk to her. Thank you, Captain Anderson, you've been helpful.'

'I'm sorry I can't do more, ma'am. Can't think how this happened. You say

16

you've had no official word? An almighty blunder. Apologies, but these things happen. Distressing all round. Tremendous volume of men and paperwork to clear. Chaotic, these last weeks.'

He began to edge away. It wasn't his department. He was responsible for discharging this trainload through Yorkshire. He'd almost got away but Private Fletcher had collared him for an explanation, but he didn't have one, apart from crass incompetence somewhere.

Hardened by his daily contact with death and disaster in the trenches he could still feel immense pity for the family who'd had all the expected joy knocked from under them. The only consolation was that somewhere up the line an unknown soldier would return from the dead list to the bosom of his mourning family. Maybe it was a similar name. Tom Ormeroyd was not uncommon in this part of Yorkshire. He spoke to the corporal's parents.

'Mr and Mrs Ormeroyd, please accept my apologies and condolences. Shocking business for you. Thank God it's ended, the war I mean.'

'Yes.'

Albert took off his bowler and wiped his forehead with a shaky hand. Bess looked awful.

Captain Anderson saluted.

'Back to the train,' he announced unnecessarily. 'Mr Ormeroyd, you'll hear from the War Department as fast as I can move 'em.'

With relief, he returned to the train.

'Mam,' Annie repeated, 'what did he mean? Tell me. What is it?'

Joan took a breath. Her daughter had to know sooner or later.

'Annie, be brave. There's been a mix-up. The wrong war records, the captain said. So much going on.'

'Yes, yes, I heard that. What about Tom?'

'Tom's not coming home. He was reported missing, believed killed. They should have told us.'

Annie stood stock still.

'Missing? But the war's over, has been for weeks. I would have known.'

She thumped her chest.

'I'd have known in here.'

She turned to Vincent.

'Did you know? You were in the same regiment.'

He nodded miserably.

'I thought you'd been told, but as Captain Anderson said it was absolute chaos. Letters weren't getting through either way and we were moved every other day or so. Besides, I didn't know what to say. Tom was like a brother and I had to get used to it. When I saw all this celebration paraphernalia, I didn't want to get off the train. When I saw you all, cheering, waving, smiling, so happy, I realised you couldn't know. You'd be glad to see me, of course, but not like you all were, excited, jubilant.'

'Watch out, she's falling.'

Jim leaped forward to catch Bess as her knees buckled.

'Best get her home,' Albert said.

'We'll catch our death out here.'

He half carried, half supported his wife.

'This'll take a bit of time to sink in. I hope you'll excuse us from the party, Joan.'

'We can't have a party now,' Jim and Joan said together.

'You must.'

Annie's voice was firm.

'Vincent's home. That's plenty to celebrate and we can have another do when Tom comes home. Go on, Mam, people will be arriving at the house. They'll not have heard about Tom. You'll have to tell them, but don't make it sad. Vincent's home,' she repeated clearly. 'Tom's posted missing.'

'Annie.' Vincent's voice was agonised. 'I saw what happened.'

'I don't want to hear now, not today. Take Mam and Dad and Meg home. We've a lot to be thankful for. You're here for us.'

'Aren't you coming home?' Meg's woebegone little voice asked shakily.

'Not just yet, love. I'm going with Uncle Albert. We'll talk about Tom, say some prayers for him.'

She went to Bess and took her other arm.

'Uncle Albert, I'll help Auntie Bess. You get a cab. There'll be one in the station yard.'

'Annie,' Joan said and her plea was torn from her heart as she watched her daughter so coolly take charge. 'Shouldn't you come home with us?'

'You've got Dad, Meg and Vincent, and all your friends and relatives at the house. Albert and Bess have no one except Tom. They need me more than you do.'

'It's not for me, it's you. I feel so much for you.'

'I'll be all right, truly. Tom's not made it for the celebration, that's all, so I don't much feel like a party. Perhaps I'll stay overnight with Auntie Bess, see how she is. I can go to work from there in the morning.'

'Work?'

Joan looked bemused. The day's events had shunted routine out of the window. It was so hard to imagine that joyful early morning and harder still to imagine Jim going off as usual in the morning to the mining offices, or Annie and Meg working in the bakery as though nothing had happened.

'Work's the answer, Mam. It'll pass the time. I'll be home tomorrow. Don't worry about me, and try to have a good time for Vincent's sake.'

Joan watched her daughter supporting Bess Ormeroyd towards the station yard where Albert held a horse-drawn cab. Shaking her head she recalled Jim's earlier words, 'This is just the beginning.'

'A poor sad beginning for our Annie,' she said to her son and husband as they, too, left the almost deserted station, 'but we'll get home, make the best of a bad job. You'll tell us about Tom, Vincent. What do you know?'

'Later perhaps, but tonight we'll put

a brave face on things, like our Annie's doing.'

Back at Nightingale Street, the Fletcher family settled for a more subdued party than they'd anticipated. Meanwhile, on the fashionable side of Castlethorpe, backed by the lush green dales, another family prepared to celebrate the return of its two sons from the war.

Hetherington Hall was a mere dozen or so miles from Nightingale Street but it could just as well have been a thousand miles away. Marcia Hetherington's knowledge of the lower end of the town was confined to charitable visits to the sick or needy, not that Marcia herself ever set foot there, but she was excellent at organising rotas for others to do so. She had a wonderful talent for organising other people's lives. Now her sons were home for good she looked forward to using her talent on their behalf.

In the grand reception hall of the main entrance, Marcia reviewed her three menfolk like a commanding general before battle. She adjusted her husband's bow tie.

'You never get it quite right, do you, dear?'

Sir William gave a sigh born of long habit.

'I try my best, and in any case you look so supremely elegant any defects we may have will be totally unnoticed.'

'Thank you, William.' The compliment was gracefully acknowledged. 'George, you are not to disappear into the billiard room after dinner. The dance will start immediately afterwards and I have a list of eligible young girls. Not too soon to plan your futures.'

'Hang on, Mother,' her younger son said and backed away in alarm. 'Ted and I have only been home a couple of days. Give us a chance for a breather, recovery time, you know.'

'It's been pretty nerve-racking, Ma, don't rush us.'

Edward Hetherington smiled affectionately at his mother but warning bells rang in his head. He'd almost forgotten how ruthless Marcia could be and a long absence from the family hearth had given him a new perspective on many things.

'I know you've suffered, particularly you, Edward, being in France so long but it's done with now, in the past. Your father and I have plans for the future and tonight's dinner and dance is just a start. Don't you go off early either. I insist you both stay to the very last dance.'

Edward shrugged his broad shoulders.

'So long as you remember George and I have been out of the social round for a while and we need time to polish up our society manners. You didn't consult us before you organised this bash.'

Marcia frowned. Edward was changed, not the same young golden boy who'd left Castlethorpe for France, a patriotic idealist eager to fight for king and country. He was much more intractable now, would need careful handling.

'Did I ever have to consult you before?' she queried.

'Times have changed, Ma. I'm four years older and a fair bit wiser.'

His smile took the sting out of the remark. His mother meant well but like most civilians she had absolutely no clue what the war had really been like. He'd miraculously survived when so many of his friends hadn't and he had to repay the debt, be useful in the life statistically he should have lost. His trench experiences were too close for him not to resent his mother so swiftly pitch-forking him into Castlethorpe's frothy social whirl.

George had served only nine months in France but he, too, was thankful to be alive. His philosophy was the reverse of his brother's and he was going to enjoy every minute of his survival and live life to the full. He'd go along with Ma's arrangements tonight but after that it'd be every man for himself!

Carriages in the driveway announced the arrival of the selected special dinner guests. Marcia flicked an imaginary speck from Edward's lapel.

'You'll do, Ted. I'm very proud of you both, and . . . um . . . so is your father,' she added as an afterthought.

'Glad to hear it.'

Ted braced himself.

'And I'd be grateful if you didn't introduce me as Major Hetherington. Ted'll do, and George and I, we don't want to talk about the war. That was a different country and not many of your guests tonight will have been anywhere near there. All right?'

'Do I have a choice?'

Marcia pursed her beautifully made-up lips.

'No.'

Ted was firm, then kissed her on the cheek in recompense.

'And Dad's right, Ma, you look smashing, a real bobby-dazzler.

'Edward! Don't be vulgar, and don't call me Ma.'

She slapped him lightly on the wrist but couldn't help a small glow of satisfaction. She was a lucky woman to have two such handsome boys and only hoped the war hadn't entirely ruined them.

The butler announced the first guests and Marcia went straight into gracious hostess mode . . .

Back on the other side of town, Albert Ormeroyd put the kettle on for what seemed to Annie the hundredth cup of tea since they'd left the bleak station. Albert's house was substantial, a suitable home for one of Castle-thorpe's bank managers. Albert and Bess, to their sorrow, had no children of their own to fill the house but Tom had been a much-cherished and precious gift.

'Bess is asleep now, poor soul. I'm that glad you came back with us, Annie. I couldn't have coped on my own.'

'I think we've helped each other. I couldn't have faced a party. It was such a shock, all that waiting, the build-up, wondering if Tom would have changed, going to the station all so excited. I can't . . . oh it was so cruel.'

She buried her face in her hands and at last gave way to her disappointed grief and wept. Albert wordlessly handed over a large snowy handkerchief. There was nothing he could do, not at this stage. He watched her tears flow until the kettle's whistle sent him into the kitchen to make tea. When he came back with the tray Annie was composed.

'I'm sorry, Uncle Albert, I just couldn't stop that. It was selfish, crying for my disappointment that he wasn't there.'

'Don't be sorry, it's natural.'

He uncorked a bottle and poured generous measures of brandy into the scalding tea.

'This'll do you good. Then we'd best get to bed. It's been a long day and you've got to be at the bakery early in the morning.'

Annie wiped her eyes and took the tea.

'I'm all right now. I shan't do that again.'

The brandy-laced tea warmed and comforted her. She put out a hand to Albert who looked ten years older since the morning.

'You mustn't give up, for Aunt Bess's sake, and mine and Tom's, too. We mustn't forget he's missing, not dead. He's a survivor. We've got to believe he's still alive. We've got to carry on or when he comes back he'll be angry if we're moping. Uncle Albert, he has such plans for the future. In his letters he has it all worked out. Did he tell you?'

Albert nodded. 'A bit, in outline. Very grand ideas our Tom always had.'

'Has. Don't speak of him in the past tense, Uncle. We've got to get on with his plans for when he comes back.'

'Annie, you mustn't kid yourself. Missing believed dead always means just that — dead.'

'No! No, don't say it. Don't believe it. Ever!'

Albert sighed. He had no statistical knowledge of how many men ever returned from the missing-believed-dead category but he didn't rate it very high. But if the belief that Tom might one day miraculously return helped Annie through the early stages of grief, then so be it.

'Drink your tea, lass, you look fair whacked. Then we'd best turn in.'

The oblivion of sleep would be a welcome release from the day, and tomorrow evening, once back in Nightingale Street, Annie knew exactly what she was going to do.

A week later, life had, outwardly at least, settled back into routine for the Fletchers. There were adjustments. Vincent at home meant the house was over-crowded. He had to sleep on the sofa in the back parlour and couldn't seem to settle on what he wanted to do. Yet again Joan raised the question of moving to one of the new houses on the edge of town. Jim as usual said he'd think on it.

Every morning, Annie and Meg set out at five o'clock for Buckby's bakery. Meg's chatter lightened the cold walk.

'Mrs Buckby's baby's due next month, her fifth. Would you want five babies, Annie? She does rely on you a lot, and Mr Buckby, too. I just love that new cherry sponge you invented.'

'I just adapted the recipe a bit. What about the fudge cake?'

'Yummee.' Meg rolled her eyes. 'All sold by mid-morning. Mrs Buckby said what would she do without you?'

'I'm glad to work hard just now.'

'Oh, Annie, I can't bear to think about . . . '

'Then don't. Here we are. I can smell the first bread batches. In you go. It'll be nice and warm in there.'

Thus the days were bearable and every evening Annie went to the room she shared with Meg and read her way very steadily through Tom's letters. Joan worried about her. Annie was too dry-eyed, too controlled, too remote.

'It's as if she's somewhere else,' she confided to Vincent, 'in another world, just going through the motions here.'

'Leave her be. It's her way of getting through this. Annie's a strong character, Mam. She always was a tough kid at school. No one'd dare fight with her, and remember how she protected Meg always.'

'This is different,' Joan insisted, 'and she's up to something, too.'

'Good for her.'

Vincent's own trench traumas had taught him the only way to maintain sanity was to learn to be self-contained and acquire a distancing technique. Pretend the horrors weren't happening and live somewhere else in your head. It didn't always work but he well under-stood what Annie was doing.

So in those early weeks, the Fletchers tiptoed around each other almost as though expecting something to happen. Annie's plan was just that — to make something happen. She had her plan in outline from Tom's letters. She filled in details from hours at the local institute and library, information gathering, building up her file.

One Friday afternoon she was ready. Slapping the last batch of dough into bread tins she took off her pinny and went to see her employer.

'I need an hour off, Mr Buckby. I've finished up the work. Meg'll see to the clearing up.'

He looked startled. Annie never took time off, not even after the sad news about Tom Ormeroyd.

'Of course, I don't grudge you time off. You've worked hard enough. Are you not well? All that business. Heard from the War Department yet?'

'No. Captain Anderson said it'd be a long time. I'm perfectly well, just have some business to see to,' Annie said firmly, and went to get her coat, leaving Mr Buckby agog with curiosity.

Meg was harder to fob off.

'Where are you going? We always walk home together.'

'We do, but not today. Alice'll go with you for company. She lives in the next street to us.'

'Is it shopping? I'd love to come.'

Annie kneeled down and took Meg's hands.

'Sort of, but I can't tell you yet. Later, I promise, and can this be our secret? Don't say anything to Mam and if I'm not home say I'm staying late at the bakery.'

'Fibs?'

Meg's eyes widened.

'Just for once, a little white one,' Annie replied.

She walked fast into town, turning up the fur collar of her coat against the bitter cold. She was nervous. What if he said no, and where would her plans go then? She mentally rehearsed her arguments. It had to work. She must find a focus for her life, until Tom came back.

The town was busy. Trams and carriages clattered over the cobbled streets, the horses pulling them snorting clouds of steamy breath into the icy air, and a few of the wonderful new motorised vehicles jostled for space, horns honking. Annie was nearly there when she stopped, panic-stricken. What on earth was she doing? It was a crazy scheme, madness! Best go home, forget all about it, live quietly, without risk. Then she thought of Tom, took a deep breath and stepped forward briskly to cross the road.

'Hey!'

'What the devil — look out.'

Annie felt a hand on her shoulder, an arm round her waist, as she was unceremoniously pulled away from the motor car swerving perilously near the kerb, and to Annie, just about to step off it. Her bag went flying, its catch burst open, and the contents tumbled to the pavement.

'Oh, no!'

She struggled to rescue her things but the hands held her steady.

'Careful now. Are you all right? George, help the lady. Can't you see those papers blowing away? Now, miss, can you stand up? That road hog all but knocked you down and he hadn't the decency to even stop and apologise. George, get his number.'

'Dashed if I can see it.'

George was still on the pavement, shuffling Annie's things into her bag.

'Please, don't. I'm all right. It was my fault. I wasn't looking where I was going,' she was protesting.

She turned to face her rescuer. Tall and fair, his overcoat and hat spoke money, but his blue-eyed smile was friendly and warm.

'You look a little shaken.'

He was well-spoken, what sister Meg would call a toff.

'Can I get you anything? There's a café over there. Maybe some tea, a glass of water?'

'Oh, no, thank you. I have an appointment at the bank. I'll be late.'

'We've just come from there. What a coincidence. George, let's have the lady's bag. Take her arm and we'll escort her up the steps.'

'No, really, I don't want a fuss.'

As Annie stepped forward she winced. Her ankle had twisted a little.

'See, you're in no state to walk. Take my arm, see how the foot bears your weight. I'm Ted Hetherington, by the way, and the keeper of your bag is my brother, George.'

'Annie Fletcher. Please let me go on. See, there's no trouble with the foot. Thank you both very much for your help.'

She took her bag from George, walked cautiously to the foot of the marble steps, and turned and smiled at the two men.

'You see, no harm done.'

Then as easily as her pained ankle allowed, she walked towards the imposing entrance of one of Castlethorpe's biggest banks and disappeared through its heavy doors. The young men stared after her.

'What an uncommonly pretty girl,' George said. 'What stunning eyes.'

'They were sad eyes,' Ted said. 'She looked as though she's lost something.'

'Could it be this dainty handkerchief?'

George winked and waved a scrap of linen in front of his brother.

'Just in case we run into Annie Fletcher again here's a good excuse. May come in handy.'

'You're outrageous, George,' Ted said and snatched the hanky. 'I'll take charge of that, just in case! I certainly wouldn't like to think of you harassing Miss Fletcher. I wonder what she's doing in the bank. All those papers she was carrying, most intriguing.'

He stared at the bank doorway as though his eyes followed Annie's progress to the counter.

3

'Come in,' Albert Ormeroyd called out but didn't look up from the column of figures, his attention held by a puzzling discrepancy in one of his junior cashier's ledgers.

He'd noted his four o'clock appointment, a Mr Fletcher, with a pencilled comment by his secretary — *insists on seeing you personally. Very insistent.* Albert closed the ledger and rose to greet the insistent Mr Fletcher.

'Good aftern ... Good heavens, Annie! Something wrong at home? I've an appointment but it can wait. It's not important.'

'Uncle Albert ... um ... Mr Ormeroyd, I'm your appointment. M. Fletcher.'

'But why?'

'I wanted to talk to you, on business, so I thought I'd come to the bank.'

'M. Fletcher — I assumed it was a man!'

'I couldn't say Annie Fletcher. I told a fib, and said I was M. Fletcher's secretary.'

Albert sat down heavily.

'Well, I'll be jiggered.'

'Your secretary wasn't too pleased to see me. I'm sorry, but I thought this was the best way.'

Albert continued to stare at her then shook his head.

'Have a seat while I get over the shock. Does your dad know you're here?'

'No one does. I wanted to talk to you first.'

'I'm flattered.'

Albert couldn't help an inward chuckle. Castlethorpe's cream one minute, with the Hetherington lads bringing a nice bit of business. He'd give his eye teeth to get the Hetherington business account! And now little Annie Fletcher. He couldn't imagine what she wanted but she was looking a bit more relaxed now. He guessed she was more nervous than she let on. Albert pressed the buzzer on his desk.

'Tea for two please, Miss Wilkes, and biscuits.'

Annie clasped her hands.

'I don't want to be a bother.'

'Calm yourself, you're no bother. Breath of fresh air in this stuffy, old place. Now, when you're ready, tell me what it's all about.'

'Well, you know, Tom, in his letters . . . and you said . . . I've been thinking about it such a lot . . . nothing else in fact. Oh, my goodness, I'd rehearsed this so well and now I can't put it into words. It's all gone to pieces. Here.'

She opened her big bag and put a file on Albert's desk.

'It's all here. My brains have flown right out of my head.'

A severe woman came in with a tea tray, glared at Annie, and put it before Albert.

'Tea as ordered, Mr Ormeroyd.'

'Thanks, Elsie. That's all.'

One more sniff of disapproval and she went out.

Albert picked up the file.

'Elsie's bark's worse then her bite, and ever since we heard about Tom she's been like an old mother hen. Now, you pour out, drink your tea, and let me glance over these papers.'

Annie sipped her tea and watched Albert flip through the pages she'd so carefully prepared. The bank was even more awesome than she'd imagined. She'd never been in one before and doubted any of her family had. Banks were for the wealthy. Families like the Fletchers were paid in cash, paid their bills in cash, and were lucky if there was a surplus to carry from one week to the next, let alone put it in a bank.

Occasionally Uncle Albert looked up at her, emitting a series of sighs.

'I'll be jiggered,' he said and scratched his head. 'Where d'you get all this from?'

'The institute, library and Tom's letters. Is it stupid? It's not possible, is it, for me any road? I've wasted your time.'

'Nay, nay, sit down. It's taking me a while to adjust. I can't believe you've worked all this out on your own — buying, selling, profit and loss, capital investment, stock control, interest rates. I'm bowled over. I've seen far worse plans from some of my customers who claim to be experienced businessmen. I'd say, from this proposal, you've got a real flair for business, Annie Fletcher. In theory any road.'

'Oh, Uncle Albert. You'll help me then? The bank will lend me the money?'

Annie's eyes lit with excitement.

'Nay, I never said that,' he said gruffly and saw her smile fade. 'I'm prepared to talk business with you though I am disappointed you didn't come to me right away.'

'Well, I didn't know what to do. Didn't seem fair to come to you at home. I thought banks loaned money for this sort of thing.'

'Ay, and charge a good rate for doing so. How do you think we can afford buildings like this one, and my grand new desk?'

'I never thought.'

Annie was crestfallen.

'Why should you, you're nought but a lass, but you'll learn, and I'll help you. I've some work to finish up here and I want a close look at these figures of yours. You go home now and I'll come round to Nightingale Street later in the evening, mebbe bring Auntie Bess. Do her good to get out, see Joan. You and I, and your dad, we'll talk business.'

Annie ran over and hugged him.

'Uncle Albert, I can't tell you how relieved I am. I was that scared of coming in here I bumped into a couple of young men outside and all my things went flying and . . .'

She kissed him on the forehead.

'Do you think it could possibly work?'

'Steady on, Annie,' Albert said

nervously. 'We'll have Miss Wilkes in here wondering what the commotion is. Don't get too excited. It's nought but an idea at this stage.'

His natural conservative caution reasserted itself. Mustn't be rash, but it was grand to see Annie lively again.

'You know this is all Tom's idea?' She grew serious. 'A business was what he was planning. Out in France he wrote that was what kept him sane, planning for the future, so it's for Tom we'll be doing it, for when he comes home!'

'Don't count on that, lass, but we'll think of him while we're working on it. You know I would have backed him any road. You'd no need of the bank.'

'I'm glad I did come. I want to be independent, and I'll pay a proper rate of interest.'

'Ay, we'll see. I don't reckon to lose money so you'll have to work hard.'

Annie gathered up her handbag and gloves.

'That's the intention, Uncle Albert. What else have I got but work?'

As she turned to say goodbye Albert saw the pain back in her eyes and had to swallow back the lump in this throat. His own grief ebbed and flowed. He was luckier than Bess because he had his work to distract him. And Annie should have something to work at, too, something of her own to build instead of slaving away for the Buckbys. The tragedy of it was she was doing it for a ghost. He pushed the thought away. One step at a time, early days yet.

That evening, Annie fingered Tom's silver ring which she wore on a fine chain round her neck and bent her head to conceal a smile. Stunned into silence her family's faces were comic studies.

Jim at last managed, 'A shop! Our Annie with a business of her own?'

Albert nodded.

'What's so strange about that? Lots of folk have shops and now the war's over there'll be plenty of families settling down again to normal life. Folk can do without luxuries but they've got to have food.'

'But Annie's no experience.'

'She'll learn, and she's a hard worker.'

Joan's eyes were lighting up.

'I can give a hand.'

'And me,' Meg piped up. 'More fun than Buckby's. All I ever do there is make the tea, sweep the floor and mind the children.'

'It's not meant to be fun,' Annie rebuked. 'It's to be a proper business. It's what Tom wants only it'll be on a bit smaller a scale to start with.'

'Our Tom's notions were a bit grand,' Albert interrupted hastily. 'He saw himself as a bit of an empire builder but I intended to help him so I'm pleased to help Annie. She's got a business head on her, worked everything out. And I've been doing a bit of research, too.'

'You might have told us, Annie,' Jim pointed out. 'Asked for our help.'

'I went to the bank, Dad, on business. I never expected . . . '

'It's very good of you, Albert,' Joan said quickly.

'Nay, I mean to make a bit of money out of it and it'll give me and Bess something to think about.'

'What'll you sell?' Meg asked.

'Groceries, everything, home-made cakes, bread . . . '

'I've found premises,' Albert broke in eagerly. 'Those new houses on t'other side of Castlethorpe. There's a parade of shops going up, double-fronted, modern, just the right spot. You can sign the lease right away, Annie, be in there in a month. No point hanging about.'

Now he had the bit between his teeth Albert wanted action.

'It's decided then, is it?'

Jim was still annoyed Annie had by-passed her own family.

'You're too young. I don't like the idea.' He dug in his heels. 'She's all right at Buckby's, and that new estate's miles away. How's she going to get there every day?'

'Dad, there's trams,' Annie exclaimed.

'There's accommodation, actually, a nice little flat over the shop, three bedrooms, inside lavatory,' Albert ventured.

'A flat! On her own? What are you thinking about, Albert Ormeroyd? I'll not have that.'

'We could all move over there.'

Joan threw in her bombshell, and it was Vincent who calmed the resulting uproar. He'd been quiet during the row, scanning through Annie's file.

'How about me renting this flat? I need a place of my own. I'll help Annie out and she can stay over if needs be.'

'How are you going to pay rent? You haven't even got a job?' Jim exploded, still fuming at Annie's rebellion.

'Yes, I have. I'm playing the piano at the Empire, for the moving pictures. I saw the manager and he's taking me on. Bit of projection work, too.'

'That'd be ideal,' Joan said. 'It'd be a proper business. Something to work for.'

'But it's for Tom.'

Annie's cry was drowned as they all started up again, talking at and across each other in excitement or anger. She didn't like the way things were going. Within an hour it looked as though her idea had been taken over.

Her mother was already listing the things they would sell, Vincent was planning the furnishings of his flat, and Albert was coaxing Jim into agreement, diplomatically asking his advice on accounting methods for shopkeepers. She stood up.

'Please, all of you, listen. I'm doing this for Tom, for when he comes home. I want you to approve and I'd like your help but, I'm sorry, it's not Fletcher's. It'd be Ormeroyd's.'

She had their attention now and the force of her emotion moved them all. No one dare suggest Tom would be returned only by a miracle. There was something about young Annie these days that was a little daunting and both Joan and Jim realised they were dealing not with their little lass but with Annie Fletcher, a young adult with plans of her own. Her mother was the first to acknowledge it.

'You're right, Annie. I'm that proud of you for planning this all on your own. You do it your way, with Albert's financial backing of course, and we'll support you in any way you say. You're the boss.'

She beamed. Annie's knees were shaky but she stayed on her feet.

'Thanks, Mam. That's settled then, we go ahead. Uncle. Open up as soon as possible and if it's all right with all of you we'll call it Ormeroyd and Fletcher.'

The night before the grand opening Annie took out Tom's letters. She knew them by heart but the feel and touch of them gave her courage. The last weeks had been exhausting but exhilarating, the setting up of Ormeroyd and Fletcher, Fine Foods, totally absorbing her. Now, in the last quiet moments of the day she recalled Tom's spirit and dedicated her future to Ormeroyd and Fletcher.

She retied the letters, pressed the packet to her lips and put them away at the back of the wardrobe. She didn't need them any more. They were in her heart, and that night she slept deep and dreamlessly for the first time since the fateful news at Castlethorpe station.

Next day, they were all ready half an hour before the official opening time, Joan, Meg and Annie. Bess was coming later with a hot lunch. Albert and Jim had to fret their way through their working day before they could join in. Annie clutched Vincent's hand.

'Doesn't it look grand? I can't wait.'

'Not so bad. You've worked like a Trojan, Annie.'

'You all have. It'll work, Vincent, won't it?'

'Just look around. Can't fail.'

He gestured towards the double-fronted windows with provisions of every kind displayed. Pretty gold lettering on the ornate window mouldings outside declared Ormeroyd and Fletcher . . . Fine Foods . . . Purveyors of Groceries and Provisions. Mahogany counters gleamed, glass cabinets sparkled. It was tasteful, eye-catching, and had the air of a high-class establishment.

'But if it fails, how could I ever pay Uncle Albert?'

'Stop worrying. It won't fail. Just look at the crowd outside. That big advertisement in The Echo looks as though it's paid off. Here we go. You open the door, Annie, it's your business.'

She crossed her fingers and as soon as the door swung open she was nearly bowled over before she could nip round to the other side of the counter for the serious shopping to begin.

'Pound of butter, four ounces of tongue, lump of cheese, and a pennyworth of humbugs.'

'Humbugs? T' other side, half a tick.'

Annie bumped into her mother

looking for sugar bags.

'This isn't sorted right. The sweets are too far from . . .'

She was back in a jiffy to her own counter.

'There you are. Mrs Green from down the road, isn't it? How's baby doing?'

'Wherever are they all coming from?' Bess exclaimed later in the morning as she pushed through to the stockroom at the back with her basket of hot pies.

'It's the novelty, I expect. First shop to open on the parade.'

'Slacking off a bit,' Joan said, flushed and beaming. 'We need more of those sweets out here. That nougat's going like hot cakes. What on earth?'

A tremendous clatter accompanied by what sounded like gun shots sent them running back into a shop which was emptying rapidly as customers dashed outside to see what was causing the commotion. Bang outside the shop a motor vehicle shuddered to a rattling halt and, as the driver and his passenger leaped out, clouds of hissing steam rose from the bonnet.

'It's going to blow up,' Bess shrieked, clutching Vincent's arm.

'Nay, it's just over-heated. They're having a bit of bother with that model. Grand looking though, ain't she?'

As the steam dispersed, the onlookers crowded round the new form of transport, still a bit of a rarity in these parts, especially such a fine-looking one. The driver took off his goggles and scratched his head.

'Dashed odd. I made sure she was topped up with water. Now what?'

He looked around, suddenly aware of his audience.

'What's this then? Quite a party. Something up?'

'New shop opening.'

A youth jerked his head towards Ormeroyd's, eyes goggling with admiration as he touched the shiny door of the motor.

'That's handy, I'll get some water.

You stay here, George. You know you really should carry a can of water.'

He took off his leather gauntlets and tossed them in the back seat.

'Now we're totally at the mercy of Ormeroyd and Fletcher, Fine Foods. I say!' he said, looking up at shop.

Customers had drifted back into the shop and Ted followed, can in hand, doing a double-take when he saw the crowded premises. He took in the extensive and varied stock, the apparently numerous assistants behind the counters, spotted the only male and made a bee line for him.

'I'm really sorry when you're so busy but when you've a minute, could I have a spot of water?'

He held up the empty can.

'Certainly. You the lucky owner of that beauty out there?'

Vincent took the can.

'Oh, no, that's my brother's. He just forgot the basic requirements. I like the way you've kitted out your shop. New, isn't it?'

'First day today, but I'm not the owner.'

He pointed across the floor.

'That's the proprietor, my sister.'

'Your sister?'

Ted searched his memory and the answer surfaced immediately.

'Why, that's the young lady at the bank. Annie, wasn't it? Annie Fletcher, of Ormeroyd and Fletcher, of course!'

Vincent nodded.

'I'll get your water if you'll wait a tick.'

'Pleasure.'

Ted's eyes were riveted on Annie, talking animatedly with a young woman. As the woman took her groceries, Annie popped a sweet in the child's mouth.

'That's for being such a good girl and helping your mam with the shopping. See you again, I hope.'

'Yes, please,' the little girl said eagerly. 'Please.'

As the woman left, Annie looked up, met Ted's gaze and started, hand to mouth, recognition instant. He moved across between the customers and held out his hand.

'Miss Fletcher, what a nice surprise. We met a few weeks ago by the bank. I've been looking out for you. Congratulations, you seem to have started something here. I confess I was guilty of thinking your brother was the owner.'

'I expect that will be a common mistake,' Annie said rather tartly. 'Mr Hetherington, isn't it? What are you doing here?'

'My brother's motor car broke down outside. Needs water. Ah, here it is. Thanks.'

He hesitated, looking from sister to brother.

'This looks a really fine business, just what the area needs. I'd like to . . . '

'Ted, get a move on. These children are climbing all over the car, the little . . . ah . . . it's the bank lady. Miss Fletcher, isn't it?'

George raised his cap. Ted handed him the can and gave him a push.

'Go on then, fill up the radiator. I'll be out in a second.'

Vincent and Annie were already back on duty. Ted waited impatiently behind a couple of women before he was face to face again with Annie.

'What? You're still here! Anything wrong, Mr Hetherington?'

'No, not at all. I'd like to talk to you, that's all.'

'Talk to me?' Annie was puzzled. 'Whatever for? And you can see I'm very busy. There's a queue behind you.'

'I'll take a jar of that marmalade then, and those chocolates, a pound of bacon, two pounds of cheese and a big bag of apples.'

Annie gave him a funny look but speedily assembled his impromptu order and rang up the till. He hadn't the air of a man who habitually shopped for groceries but she took his money and smiled politely. He was very attractive, as tall as Tom, with the same thick fair hair, but his eyes were blue, Tom's more grey-blue.

'Thank you,' she said. 'Next.'

'Miss Fletcher, may I call again?'

Ted bundled the bag under his arm.

'We'd be pleased to have your custom, but I should guess it's out of your way.'

'No matter, I'd like to see how things go.'

'Well, I can't stop you, but I don't see why . . . '

'Ted!'

The anguished roar from outside finally made him move.

'To the next time then, Miss Fletcher. Good luck with Ormeroyd and Fletcher, Fine Foods.'

Annie stared after him for a second, then turned her attention to her next eager customer.

4

Joan Fletcher stopped short in the doorway of Ormeroyd and Fletcher, Fine Foods and said, 'Now what? I know you've a weakness for sweeties but this is ridiculous.'

'It is a bit crowded but I had to use all the work space I could find, and these aren't for me. Here, try this one and tell me what you think.'

Annie picked up a pink square of coconut candy.

'I'm going to sell all this in the shop. The kiddies gave me the idea. I always pop them a sweet to stop them grizzling while the mums are shopping. That soon ran down the stock so I thought why not make my own? Good profit and no wastage.'

'You always did have a way with toffees. This one's delicious but you're overdoing it. You must be exhausted.'

'No, I love it. Vincent says I should make lots more and he'll try them in the market.'

'But you've so much to do. You practically live in the shop and we've scarcely seen you in Nightingale Street these last weeks.'

'I know but I do see you here most days and I've been sorting out recipes. I'm best being busy.'

For a moment her excited eagerness dropped away and sadness clouded her dark eyes. Joan moved towards her.

'Annie, love, if making a ton of toffees keeps you from thinking about Tom then I'm with you. I just don't want you to kill yourself with work.'

'That's not likely. I'd not be much use to Tom then.'

Joan bent to examine the different varieties of toffees. No use pointing out that Tom was unlikely to return. It was nearly four months since they'd all set out to meet Vincent and Tom and there'd been no word from the War

Department in spite of Albert's badgering them. They all knew Tom wasn't coming back. Only Annie stuck to the hope he was alive somewhere in Europe and would one day return to claim his faithful sweetheart.

Such was the gulf between Annie and her family on this it was now almost impossible to mention Tom at all. Joan sighed and concentrated on her daughter's latest scheme.

'It's real good quality stuff, homemade taste. You'll do well with it.'

'You know I couldn't manage without you and Meg, and Vincent of course, but he wants to work more at the Picture House.'

'I like it. Gives me something to do though your dad's not best pleased. Can't get used to women running things. Not natural, he says.'

Annie laughed.

'Poor Dad, he'll have to get used to changes. Uncle Albert's all for it.'

'Well, I'd best bustle down to the shop and give Meg a hand. It's Friday, our busiest day.'

'That'd be champion. I'll be able to pack these up for tomorrow's market, and Vincent says maybe we can sell to other shops later on.'

'Goodness me, it'll be a proper big business soon.'

'That's what Tom wants. He has grand plans.'

Joan pursed her lips. Much as she'd liked Tom and had approved of their romance she couldn't help a twinge of irritation at the way his ghost constantly hovered over the shop, but wisely all she said was, 'I'll go down then.'

'Give me a shout if you need me.'

Once Joan had gone, Annie worked swiftly bagging and labelling the sweets.

'It must work, it must,' she breathed.

Already her imagination was spinning to marzipans, fondants, nougats and brittles, crystallised fruits for Christmas, Easter eggs, butterscotch, fudges, endless things to do to fill the vacant time until Tom came back to claim his empire.

'Annie, Annie.' Meg's hiss broke into her fantasies. 'He's here again, that gentleman, Mr Hetherington. He wants to see you.'

'I'm busy. Tell him to go away.'

'Why? He's so nice. We don't need you in the shop.'

'I've got all these sweets to pack up and . . . '

'I'll help, I'll stay over.'

'I shan't keep you,' the voice cut across the sisters' conversation.

'There's quite a crowd in the shop, Meg. Best go and help your mother.'

'I'll go.'

Annie reached for her shop pinafore as Meg left reluctantly, but Ted's broad frame filled the doorway, blocking Annie's way.

'Don't be cross but you're never in the shop these days. I wondered . . . my word what's this?'

His eyes swept over the boxed and loose sweets.

'What a splendid range. You didn't make them, did you?'

66

'I did, and why not?' Annie said, on the defensive.

'Why not indeed?'

Ted smiled at her, perfectly at ease in the tiny, candy-crammed kitchen.

'I should think you need a break. The car's outside, come for a drive.'

'I've got work to do. We can't all afford to take holidays.'

'I'm not suggesting a holiday, just an hour off.'

'What for?'

'Talk to you, get to know you, and what you're doing here.'

He gestured towards the sweets.

'It's magnificent.'

Annie flushed.

'Don't make fun of me. It's only a few homemade things.'

'Looks more like a small factory to me.'

'It's just an experiment, and I wish you'd go, Mr Hetherington. You really shouldn't be here at all. I'm going to take these boxes down to the shop.'

'All right. I'll give you a hand.'

He took a dozen boxes and stepped aside to let her pass.

'But I'll call again.'

'No. No, you mustn't, there's no point. It's impossible.'

They were now in the shop, crowded with customers, many of whom looked curiously at Ted, recognising him as the elder son of Hetherington's Jams and Pickles, one of the largest employers in Castlethorpe. Few could imagine why he was on this side of town let alone coming down the stairs of Fletcher's Foods. Customers gawped and murmured as he left the shop.

'I reckon he's sweet on our Annie,' Meg said unwisely then shrank back in alarm as her idolised older sister turned on her.

'Don't say such a stupid thing. It's not true. Now, next please.'

The noise level resumed and Annie's hot face cooled. Later she said sorry to Meg for snapping but it was only when the shop was closed much later in the evening that she knew what she should have done. It was obvious that she should have said to Ted that she was sorry, it wouldn't be right to go for a drive because she was engaged to be married to Tom Ormeroyd.

★　★　★

Ted tilted his chair backwards to look out of the library's stone-mullioned windows. The bright spring sunshine was far more enticing than Uncle Jack's weekly rundown of the firm's accounts. George was glaze-eyed, Sir William vaguely and politely interested, only Lady Marcia was enthralled.

'So in this financial quarter profits show a steady upward movement, jams and pickle sales being in direct ratio to . . .'

'Uncle Jack, we've got this on paper,' George said weakly. 'Do we have to go through it line by line?'

'Yes, we do,' Jack Hetherington said sharply. 'That's how business is run, constant vigilance, eyes everywhere.'

'I don't see why. The whole show runs on its own since the war. It's a seller's market.'

George folded his arms gloomily. He'd promised to go riding with Caroline in half an hour. Fat chance at this rate.

'Don't be rude to your uncle.'

Marcia's voice was whiplash. She could do without George's obvious lack of commitment at this stage of her plans. Sir William intervened.

'Let's take the finance report as read. Nothing else? Let's call it a day.'

'Not yet. I have something to say,' Marcia said quickly.

Jack shot her a bleak look. His sister-in-law was out for power and he didn't approve of that at all. He and his brother, Will, had been glad of her help during the war years, damned useful at first, but instead of fading gracefully away in the background now it was all over she insisted on a regular seat on the board. Now there was no shifting her and William didn't seem to care one way or the other.

'Meeting closed,' he said firmly.

Marcia ignored him.

'Two points. Ted and George need permanent positions on the board. So far they've attended on an ad hoc basis, picking up the threads, and we need to regularise the situation. When William retires someone must be ready-groomed to take over.'

'I'm a long way from retirement,' William spluttered.

'What about my boys? And I've a few more years after Will, don't forget,' Jack said angrily.

Ted cut across the argument.

'Don't we have a say? I can't speak for George but I've made it clear over the past year that I'm not joining Hetherington's Jams.'

'Oh, that was just some nonsense while you were in France. You have to settle down now, join the firm, marry some suitable girl. Chloe Benson for instance — pots of money, well connected.'

'Thanks, Ma, but I think I'm old enough to plan my own future, and Chloe Benson has no part of it, nice girl though she is. Thing is, out there, George and I, we didn't think we had much of a future, but we've been given one and I'm going to use it properly.'

'But you can't leave Hetherington's,' Marcia snapped. 'You've done well these last weeks.'

'It was only ever temporary and you know I never intended to stay on.'

'I need you to take care of my project.'

'What project? Now what have you done? You've no business.'

Jack glared at her as he posed the question.

'I've done nothing, yet, but I've been working on an idea, the launch of a new section in the company.'

'What, for heaven's sake, woman?' Jack exploded.

'Increase our confectionery output, chocolate, sweets, high-class confectionery, but now aim for the luxury trade. Edward, what's so funny? Jack, you'll have a heart attack in a minute. What's so outrageous?'

In the ensuing uproar, Edward, still laughing, walked out of the library.

'Settle it between you,' he called out from the doorway. 'I'll be keen to hear the outcome but count me out from now on.'

George could fight his own battles, but meanwhile he had a different challenge to face and it was nothing to do with jams or pickles.

★   ★   ★

Annie's head whirled with ideas as she walked from the shop to Nightingale Street. There was an old cook book of her grandmother's somewhere in the house and she remembered a mouth-watering section on sweets which she just had to have to add to her collection. A modern accurate sugar thermometer was essential, more trays, bigger pans, oh, so many things. She was so absorbed she didn't notice the motor vehicle until it had passed her and pulled up ahead. Ted was out in a flash, cap raised.

'Miss Fletcher, I'm glad I caught you. I called at the shop but your mother said you were on your way to Nightingale Street. Hop in, I'll take you there.'

'You again, Mr Hetherington. Thanks but I'm enjoying the walk.'

'It'll save you time and I'm sure you're busy.'

He hit the right spot. The sooner she got that book the sooner she could start cooking.

'All right then. Thank you.'

Gingerly she stepped on the running-board as Ted opened the passenger door. She'd never been in one of these things before. It was surprisingly comfortable but she clutched her hat in alarm as the motor jerked forward.

'Sorry, a bit unpredictable as yet.'

Ted concentrated on steering and Annie began to enjoy the sensation of watching the world go by from the front seat of an open tourer.

'So, how are things going?'

'Things?'

'The sweet making.'

'Very well. I can't keep up with demand.'

'That's good.'

'Not really. It's frustrating, particularly as there's such a wide-open market. I've orders I can't meet.'

Ted looked at her fine profile, saw the furrow in her brow, noted a paleness from fatigue that hadn't been there when he first bumped into her by the bank. She intrigued him enormously but there was a protective force around her which warned off closer contact. He had to be very careful.

'I expect you need more equipment to produce on a larger scale, and perhaps proper premises.'

'Why, that's right.'

She turned her full face to him and her wide smile touched his nerves.

'You understand that. No one else

seems to. They all think I should be content with the shop. I'm not.'

Ted kept a firm grip on the wheel.

'I'd like to show you something. Only a small detour.'

'What for? What is it? I can't . . . '

'You'll see, hang on.'

He swung the car off the main road, crossed a couple of streets and turned up a rutted lane.

'Mr Hetherington,' Annie said, clutching the sides of the car as it bounced unevenly down the track, 'we should turn back. I haven't time . . . '

'We're here.'

He stopped and came round to open the door.

'Just a step, over that bridge.'

He strode off and she had to follow, frowning. Under the bridge, a clear brown stream ran through lush meadow.

'I didn't know this place existed. It's so near town yet it could be in the heart of the country.'

'George and I used to come here

before all the houses were built. It's part of a farm belonging to the estate.'

'The Hetherington Estate?'

'Yes.'

'It's a long way from the Hall.'

'Not so far as the crow files,' he said easily. 'Come down to the stream. There are wild flowers farther along, primroses, violets.'

'I shouldn't.'

'Come on. It's a beautiful spring day. The air'll do you good.'

He stopped, face raised to the sun. Annie looked away quickly as he spoke with quiet intensity.

'If you only knew how many times in that never-ending sea of mud and rain I conjured up this scene, all the different seasons but especially now, spring. It kept me sane.'

'You were in France? How long?'

'Through the war, four years, but that's done with now, in the past. Now's important, so come and walk with me.'

He held out a hand and slowly she

put out her hand to meet it.

'Just a little way then, and only if you tell me about France,' she said.

His hand fell back.

'Must I? I want to forget it.'

His blue eyes searched her face until she flushed under his scrutiny and looked down at the mossed cobbles on the bridge.

'All right then, just this once.'

He took her arm and led her down to the water and for a while they walked in silence.

'See the primroses in the hedgerows on the far bank? There are kingcups, too.'

'It must be strange after so long, coming back to all this, for good.'

'I'm just thankful, and grateful, that I did come back.'

Annie felt her heart pound, breathing difficult. She put her hand to her throat. The pulse was racing strongly and the cry was forced from her.

'Tom hasn't come back, yet.'

It was out! Her heart subsided. Ted

didn't slacken his pace.

'Tom?'

'Tom Ormeroyd, my fiancé. He's still missing. He wasn't on the train. We didn't know. Some officer said . . . '

'You went to the station expecting to meet him?'

She nodded.

'That must have been terrible. What did the officer tell you?'

'That Tom was missing, believed dead, but it's not true. He'll come back. That's why I'm doing the sweets, for Tom. He always wanted a business.'

She tailed off and stared at the water. Ted was silent. Her arm was still in his, her face averted. He knew the odds. As an officer he'd lived with their consequences long enough.

'It's possible, isn't it? You'd know. Weren't you an officer? People have come back.'

He put both hands on her shoulders and turned her to him.

'In my experience, it's very unlikely

he . . . Tom . . . will come back. I'm so sorry, Annie, but I'd be lying if I told you otherwise.'

She felt the strength of his fingers yet despite his words hope flowed through her. She liked and trusted him, he was sincere, but wrong. They all were, but in a curious way she was strongly drawn to this man who'd practically delivered Tom's death sentence. She wanted him to hold her closer and for a second closed her eyes and imagined what it would be like. His voice came from 'way off.

'Annie, are you all right?'

She swayed a little then opened her eyes. He was still there, reassuring.

'Yes. Yes, I am. I'm glad you brought me here. It's calming.'

'We'll come again, follow the river, bring a picnic.'

'Perhaps, so long as you remember about Tom.'

'I understand that, but we can be friends.'

Annie considered this strange notion.

In spite of the obvious gaps between them she felt at ease with him. He must know something about business, too. Her family was scared to death of expanding. Ted could advise her, and he'd been in France for four years and that was a connection with Tom.

'All right.'

She held out her hand and Ted shook it gravely.

'Fine. Now I'll take you home.'

He'd made a small dent in her armour and that would have to be enough for now.

As soon as Annie let herself into the house she knew something was wrong. Joan and Meg were in the front parlour with Albert and Bess.

Albert said, 'I picked your mother and Meg up from the shop.'

He held out a letter to her.

'It's finally come through from the War Department, official confirmation about Tom.'

'Sit down, love, I'll make some tea,' Joan said and looked anxiously at Annie as she unfolded the paper to read its brief contents.

To her amazement Annie was smiling.

'Uncle Albert, we know this. Missing, believed killed — not dead. They can't know that because they haven't got his body.'

'You've got to stop this, Annie. Bess and I accept Tom's dead. You must, too.'

'I won't. You'll see, Tom'll walk in here one day large as life and he won't want to be met with a lots of long faces. Now, I'm going to find Granny's old cook book. I've got a feeling it's in one of those boxes in the shed.'

Joan made to follow her but Bess held her back.

'Leave her be. She'll deal with it in her own time. It's her way of coping and it can't do her any harm. Indeed, from what Albert says, it's going from strength to strength. You'll see, it'll all turn out for the best.'

'I wish I could believe you,' Joan said.

5

Albert Ormeroyd noted the change with satisfaction. As on her first visit, Annie sat opposite his imposing desk but now there was no sign of the shy tentativeness of two years earlier. As she leaned forward to tap the pile of papers on the desk her voice had the ring of authority.

'You see, Uncle, as we are, still over the shop, I can't move forward. I've a mountain of orders which I can't hope to fill and there's so much unexplored territory. I need another salesman, and premises. There's a small factory for lease on the outskirts of Castlethorpe, Chappells, they're moving out. It'd be grand, just right, reasonable terms.'

Albert held up his hand.

'Whoa! The bank'll likely back you but I need to put these figures to head office. I want you to be sure you're doing the right thing. You're going along very nicely as you are, tidy profit last year. With this scheme, if it works, you'll be moving into a bigger league, more risks, more borrowing.'

'I know, I know, and I have thought about it. I can do it. Ted says . . . '

'Ted? Hetherington, I suppose?'

'Yes, and why not? He knows about business even though he's not in the family firm and he reckons it's the right thing to do.'

'Well, of course, if Ted Hetherington's given it the thumbs up . . . '

'Uncle Albert, don't be sarcastic. Ted's a good friend.'

Albert gathered up the papers.

'Be that as it may, I'll let you know soon.'

'Sooner, please. I want to get on right now. I've advertised for a Master Sweetmaker so before I can offer a job I need to know if I can go ahead, confirm that new equipment.'

'Looks as though your mind's made

up so I'll have to persuade head office. Tea?'

'No thanks, Uncle, I'd love to but I'm . . . er . . . meeting Ted and I've a stack of things to see to.'

She cast down her eyes to avoid Albert's shrewd, questioning gaze. Albert said nothing. No point mentioning the rumours flying about the town. Annie was no fool. Rumours didn't worry her. Her purpose in life was clear. In less than two years she'd transformed Ormeroyd and Fletcher, Fine Foods, into Northern Candy, a name to be reckoned with in the wholesale sweet trade.

Albert couldn't recall how and why the name had changed but privately speculated that if by some miracle Tom returned from the dead he'd be hard put to recognise the little Annie he'd left behind as the confident, young woman before him now. He sighed as he pulled the latest of Annie's future predictions folder towards him.

'Uncle Albert,' she said softly, 'you

know this is all for Tom, don't you? Just think how pleased he'll be.'

Albert swallowed. She had the most uncanny knack of reading his mind. They hardly ever spoke of Tom now. Everyone apart from Annie accepted he was dead, buried in some forgotten corner of France.

'Don't worry, Uncle, I know what you all think, but I still believe he'll come back. Otherwise why would I go on? You'll see one day.'

She dropped a kiss on his cheek.

'You're wonderful, Uncle Albert, and Tom'll thank you for it one day.'

Albert saw her out and for a long time after he sat staring at her facts and figures. She was so shrewd, yet so blinkered on this one thing. He and Bess knew they'd lost a precious son but Albert had a formidable business partner and he had to admit he loved the challenge of Northern Candy with all its problems.

★ ★ ★

'Pheasant? I've never had it.'

Annie scanned the elaborate menu doubtfully.

'Perhaps you should order, Ted.'

'All right. I'm sure you'll love it, and if you don't, I'll eat yours. I've been starved of decent food these past months.'

Ted had been on a trip to Africa to report on drought and poverty in its remote regions. He was thinner than Annie remembered.

'Was it really awful?' she asked.

'Not so bad for me, but terrible for the native population. I feel so guilty, knowing all the time my deprivation was only temporary and I would come home to all this.'

He gestured towards the menu, the attentive waiters, the general atmosphere of discreet luxury.

'Pie and chips at Jim's would've done me. With what this'll cost I reckon I could buy a spanking new sugar boiler,' Annie exclaimed as she studied the wine list in horrified amazement. 'How on earth they've got the nerve to charge such a price for a bottle of wine . . . what're you laughing at?'

'You, Annie. I've never taken a girl out who'd check the price of dinner against a sugar boiler.'

'It's not a case of being taken out. We're friends and I'll pay my share.'

Annie spoke sincerely but her heart couldn't deny its pleasure at seeing Ted again after a five-month absence. She'd missed him more than she cared to admit, missed his down-to-earth approach to her plans for Northern Candy, indeed her whole business plan presented to Uncle Albert was based on Ted's calculations, and she'd agreed to dine with him at the posh Grand Hotel to tell him about her interview with Albert.

'So, he thinks the bank will agree. Isn't that good news? I say, this pheasant really is good. You were absolutely right, Ted.'

Ted couldn't take his eyes off her

expressive face. So many times that image had sustained him through the last few months just as, he reminded himself, Tom Ormeroyd must have been sustained in equally appalling conditions of human misery. And she still believed Tom would come back. He knew that. The untouchable force was still around her, a force he couldn't break through, as yet.

'Try this wine,' he said, keeping his tone casual.

'You're too pale. Working too hard?'

'Don't you start, please. Mam and Dad never stop, though Mam's been better since she's been working full time at Northern Candy, and Meg, too. She's learned secretarial and book-keeping, and Mam'll keep the factory staff in order once we're in full production. Don't you see, it'll be champion!'

'I see,' Ted said quietly, pouring more wine.

'Ted, I'm sorry, I'm so selfish, running on about Northern Candy when you've had such a dreadful time. I read your reports in the newspapers. They were so good. I hope something can be done for those poor people.'

'Maybe.' Ted shrugged. 'Just so people realise how lucky we are here although we have vast problems here, especially unemployment.'

Annie interrupted eagerly.

'Northern Candy will provide jobs at least. I'm going to be able to employ lots of people.'

Ted laughed.

'I knew we couldn't keep away from Northern Candy for long. It will provide employment and that's good but could we just forget it for a moment? Whatever you say, I'm treating you to this dinner, and I want to ask you something.'

'And I'm enjoying it. It's lovely, and it's so good to see you. I've missed you, our walks, our talks.'

'Have you?'

Ted looked at her intently.

'Of course. I rely on you a lot, you

know that. What was it you wanted to ask me?'

Ted waited until their plates were removed.

'George is getting married next month. He would like you to come to the wedding.'

Annie regarded him with astonishment.

'What would I be doing at a Hetherington wedding?'

'I'd like you to be there, meet my family.'

'Whatever for?'

Annie looked bemused. Ted swallowed his exasperated retort.

'We're friends, Annie. I thought that was understood.'

'Yes, but your brother's wedding is for family and your sort of friends.'

'For heaven's sake, what does that mean? Do you have to keep friends in separate compartments?'

' 'Course not. I don't have to, they're all like me, apart from you that is.'

'So, don't you think we need to shake

up those old ideas? Times have changed since the war.'

'I suppose.'

The waiter wheeled a trolley to their table and began a complicated routine with a small copper pan and a bowl of batter. Annie jumped when blue flames jumped up.

'What the heck?'

The waiter looked down his nose.

'Crêpes suzettes, madam, and Mr Hetherington ordered.'

'Not so well known in my circle,' Annie said wryly, 'but I'm sure they'll taste champion, and I think it's given me the idea for a new line,' she said, sniffing appreciatively.

'Annie, you're incorrigible! Coffee and liqueurs in the lounge?'

'No thanks. It's been grand but I've a hard day tomorrow. I'm interviewing for a new salesman. Vincent's so busy at the picture palace. I dread the day he'll want to leave Northern Candy.'

'Just you interviewing?'

'Just me. Why not?'

'No reason,' Ted said wisely, 'just interested.'

He beckoned for the bill.

'So you'll come to George's wedding? I'll send an official invitation.'

'I'll think about it. It's kind of you, but probably not. Now, can I tell you about an idea I had for the new factory layout?'

'If you must, but in that case we might just as well talk over coffee and liqueurs.'

'All right,' Annie agreed.

It was wonderful to have Ted on her side. She just might go to the wedding, but what on earth would she wear?

In the end, Annie compromised and agreed to go to the evening ball after the main ceremony, thinking she would be less conspicuous after the main event. She agreed to go out of a sense of obligation to Ted and a desire to see how the other half of Castlethorpe lived. She'd been egged on by her mother and Meg. The question of what to wear was solved by Joan who dug out her own wedding dress of soft cream silk and remodelled it. A dark blue bolero jacket completed the outfit and Annie was pronounced fit for any company in Castlethorpe and beyond.

Lady Marcia took a different view before she'd even set eyes on Annie. George's marriage was ideal and nothing should spoil her pleasure. The bride was entirely suitable. Caroline Langhurst was money and aristocracy and one day their fortunate first son would be in line for a baronetcy. George was pushing the family up a notch from their trade origins.

Ted was a different matter, with his odd way of life and choice of companions. His casual remark that he was bringing some unknown girl called Annie Fletcher to the wedding struck a cold blow to her pride.

'Annie Fletcher? What a common name. There are no county Fletchers surely? What's her family? Who is she?'

'Annie Fletcher is Annie Fletcher. She's a unique girl and a good friend of mine. I'd like you to meet her.'

'But at George's wedding? Must I? Whatever will Lady Langhurst think?'

'I don't much care about Lady Langhurst, and don't be such a snob.'

Marcia had to give in. With any luck no one would notice the girl, whoever she was. Lady Hetherington dismissed the matter from her mind.

As soon as Annie got out of the car Ted had sent to collect her she knew it was a mistake to have agreed to come. The women in front of her shimmered in stylish satin, fur-trimmed wraps. The blue bolero jacket much admired at home was all wrong. The high-pitched chatter and laughter denoted groups of familiar friends who all moved in the same social circle. One or two cast puzzled glances at her as Ted greeted her.

'I should never have come. I'm out of place,' she said sharply as a maid took her jacket.

'Nonsense, you look lovely,' Ted said and grasped her arm. 'Come on, Annie, believe in yourself, just as you do at Northern Candy. You're the boss there, have confidence.'

'It's different there. I'm a sham here. It's all a pretence.'

'Rubbish. I'm surprised at you. I thought you had more guts.'

All right, she'd show him, and them. Although her dress was home-made and her hair had never had a professional cut, she'd nothing to be ashamed of, and how many of those smartly-dressed women could turn out a superb batch of coconut candy? Most of them had never done a hand's turn in their life. She took a deep breath and, head held high, walked alongside Ted as he introduced her easily to people. Their nods were pleasant, friendly, even warm. She began to relax.

Lady Marcia, Sir William, the bride and groom, stood in a reception line outside the ballroom. Lively dance music set Annie's feet tapping. Ted smiled at her.

'I bet you're a great dancer.'

'I haven't had much practice lately but Tom and I . . . we used to go to the local dances when he came home on leave.'

'I'm rusty, too, so we'll make a good pair.'

Ted's hand tightened under her elbow as they reached the head of the line. Lord and Lady Langhurst were charming and Annie began to look forward to the evening as they moved towards Ted's parents.

'Mother, Father, Caroline, this is my friend, Annie Fletcher. Annie, you know George already.'

'She does?' the bride said, looking startled.

'I certainly do.'

George stepped forward, and kissed her.

'How do you do?'

Caroline followed her husband's lead. If George knew the girl that was enough for her.

'Mother?' Ted prompted as Marcia made no move to greet Annie, simply gave her a hard, assessing stare followed by the merest frosty flicker of acknowledgement.

Sir William frowned but before he could say a welcoming word Marcia hooked her arm in his and moved swiftly into the ballroom.

'Come along, William, it's high time George and Caroline started up the dancing officially. Ted, perhaps you'd join us later.'

The snub could not have been more pointed. Annie flushed scarlet.

'Mother!' Ted called angrily, but Lady Marcia's rigid back was already surrounded by guests in the ballroom.

George looked embarrassed.

'I say, Annie, I'm sorry but Ma . . . she means well, but . . . '

'That's well meaning?' Annie said furiously. 'I see exactly how your ma is. Ted, I told you this was a mistake. Times have not changed at Hetherington Hall one little jot. I'm going home, if you'd call me a cab.'

'Annie, don't be silly. I'll take you,

but I'd rather you stayed.'

'What? After your mother's behaviour? There's no point. As your mother's demonstrated so clearly we're simply not in the same league and never will be.'

6

Annie walked through the main production room of the new factory enjoying the rich buttery smell. White-overalled girls, hair neatly tucked under gauze caps, nodded acknowledgement as she greeted each one by name. She couldn't help a thrill of pride as she went into her small office.

Her achievement, Northern Candy, was up and running at last, a proper business with ever-rising sales figures. This was her empire. This was where she belonged, with her own kind, workers! In the next room her mother and Meg shared an office and beyond that her father supervised accounts and ledgers. Raymond Bell, her senior salesman, was already waiting to go over the first month's sales figures. He stood up as she came in.

'Hello, Annie. My you're looking

pretty today. That frock suits you.'

She frowned. She wasn't too sure about Raymond. He was a wonderful salesman and had already extended Northern Candy's sales into Lancashire, and had sights set beyond. She knew he was ambitious and that had to be good, but lately he'd taken to complimenting her on her appearance, brushing her arm, touching her shoulder accidentally. Even now his chair was much too close, his head almost touching hers as he leaned towards her, scanning the columns of figures.

'See,' he said as he stabbed the graph, 'that's the new account in Leeds. They're dealing solely with us now, even dropped Hetherington's to give us a good window display. How's that?'

Annie warmed towards him. Marcia's snub still rankled.

'That's good. I'd like to knock a hole in Hetherington's trade.'

Raymond moved closer, his hand touching hers.

'I'd like us . . . '

'Annie!' a familiar voice interrupted.

'Why, Ted! What a surprise.'

Annie was relieved. She hadn't seen Ted for a week, and he was a perfect excuse to send Raymond packing.

'All right, Raymond, those figures look fine. Carry on the good work. Aren't you off to Blackpool today?'

'Tomorrow.'

'I'll see you when you get back. Good luck.'

Raymond Bell put a private but virulent curse on Ted Hetherington as he stowed his samples in the back of his new car. He was good at selling but he'd no intention of remaining a commercial traveller for much longer. Raymond had big plans, for the future, and he saw Northern Candy as the ideal opportunity to further his ambitions. Ted Hetherington was a nuisance.

Meanwhile, Ted had sat down on the edge of Annie's desk.

'How are things going?'

'Fine. Sales are climbing all the time.'

'Good.'

'So why not have a break today? I've an assignment in the Dales, a piece on sheep farming. Come with me. We'll take a picnic. It's a lovely day.'

'Ted! I can't just walk out of my office and take a day off. What sort of example would that be? And, I've got to see Arthur Smee about a new line.'

'What's that?'

'Top secret, but I'll tell you Hetherington's won't be too pleased.'

'Good. The firm's getting too complacent and they need a shake up. I'll take you out to dinner tonight then. I'll pick you up at seven o'clock.'

'I'm working late, really, but I should be through by seven. Pick me up here. I've got a posh frock in the cupboard.'

'You don't need a posh frock. You're fine as you are.'

Unexpectedly he leaned over and kissed her on the cheek. For a second Annie held her breath. His lips were firm and warm.

'Tonight,' he said softly, 'and by the way, watch out for Raymond Bell. I never did approve of your choice there.'

'What business is that of yours?' she spluttered. 'I don't tell you how to do your job.'

'Ah, but I don't ask you to. See you tonight.'

After he'd gone, Annie remained at her desk but made no effort to start the day's paperwork. It was true, she'd come to rely more and more on Ted's opinion. She enjoyed talking over new ideas, but since George's wedding day they'd talked mainly business and that closeness she'd felt on their first walk together had vanished. Today, as he'd kissed her, she'd felt that shadow of intimacy again.

The day flew by and it was well past six o'clock before she felt able to leave the factory floor and go back to her office to clear her desk. She wasn't pleased to see Raymond Bell sitting in her chair, casually leafing through papers on her desk.

'Raymond, what are you doing? Those are none of your business.'

Totally unabashed, he gave her a crooked smile.

'I've been thinking I ought to take more of an interest in the administration of the firm.'

'Whatever for? Your job is sales, and very good you are, too, and I'd prefer it if you stick to that. Now, I've got a few things to clear. I'll see you when you get back from Lancashire.'

He stood up and came towards her.

'Annie, this is all too much for a young girl like you. You need a man to take charge. I've been watching you these past weeks and you're looking too pale. I could put the colour back in your cheeks.'

To Annie's utter amazement he put his arms around her and brought his mouth crushing down on hers. She tried to push him away but his grip tightened. With all her force she shoved him off so violently he hit his head against the wall.

'Don't you dare,' she gasped. 'Have you gone completely mad?'

'Aw, come on, don't play hard to get. You need a man, Annie.'

He came towards her again. This time she was ready for him. Picking up a heavy ruler she struck him full on the cheek.

'Stop it! Don't dare come any closer. You're out of a job, Mr Bell, from now. You forfeit your notice period. I'll pay you a month's wages and don't set foot on my premises again. And listen carefully, I don't need a man because I have one, a man who'd demolish you in seconds, a man who fought for the likes of you.'

'You don't mean the bloke killed in the war, Tom somebody? I heard rumours, but you can't be daft enough to believe he'll walk through the door one day. He's dead, and you must be mad to go on wasting your life. All right, all right, I'm going. I misjudged it, that's all, no crime in that, and you can keep your precious self for that rotting corpse somewhere in France.'

He slammed the door violently.

Annie sat down, horrified and shaken to the core. How could she have misjudged the man so completely? He was a good salesman and she'd often praised him warmly. Had he taken that for something else? She buried her face in her hands. It was horrible! She remembered the look in his eyes as he came towards her. She tried to blot it out by recalling Tom's face, and she couldn't, couldn't see him at all. Her anguished cry tore at Ted's heart as he opened the door.

'Annie! What's the matter? What's happened?'

In two strides he had her in his arms, held her close, stroked her hair.

'Was it to do with Bell? I saw him running through the factory.'

'Oh, he tried to . . . to kiss me . . . I didn't realise . . . and now I've lost my best salesman, but, oh, Ted, it wasn't what he did. He said Tom was dead, a rotting corpse somewhere in France. He isn't, is he? Tom's still alive. I know it, otherwise why would I be doing all this work for Northern Candy?'

Ted sat her down, pulled out a large handkerchief and passed it to her.

'I can't forget what he said about Tom. It's not true, is it, Ted?'

Her eyes, still wet with tears, pleaded with him to agree, to soothe, to reassure. Ted stayed silent.

'Ted, tell me. You must, please.'

He took her hands in his then said quietly, 'Annie, you asked me that before, on our first walk by the river. Remember?'

She nodded, feeling her hands safe in his, remembering him holding her.

'That was three years ago, and the answer's the same. I cannot honestly say I believe there's the remotest chance that your Tom is alive today. It's been too long, Annie, and I think it's time you faced the truth and moved forward in your life.'

'What do you mean, move forward? Do you mean allow people like that horrible Raymond Bell to say such things to me?'

'Of course I don't. But there are other men, good men.'

He tried to choose his words carefully. It would be too easy to go along with Annie's fantasy but someone had to shock her back into life, into a proper emotional life, before she froze totally.

'There are other men who would love you and whom you could love in return.'

Now Annie sprang away from him. Even Ted was against her. No one believed in Tom's return, no one.

'You'll see, one day you'll all be proved wrong. I'm sorry, Ted, it's been a hard day. I think I'd better go home. I don't feel like dinner.'

'You really do believe Tom's still alive after all this time?'

'Of course.'

Ted sighed. Sooner or later he would have to face the truth that Annie's heart was lost to a dream, but not yet, not just yet. He took her in his arms.

'I'll take you home then. I won't be

seeing you for a while. Tonight was going to be a farewell dinner.'

'Farewell?'

'For a while. I have to go to Europe, dispatches from Germany. I need to live there.'

'How long?'

'I don't know.'

'I'll miss you.'

'Maybe. You'll be too busy running Northern Candy.'

He looked down at her. She was such a mixture, one moment the hard-headed businesswoman, and now with her dreams of Tom, the young innocent so vulnerable. He kissed her gently on the mouth. As he felt her sweetness he could almost believe the cause was not quite lost.

Not yet, he repeated to himself, not just yet.

7

The Raymond Bell episode taught Annie she couldn't deal with every aspect of running a growing business. Her mother Joan was a shrewd judge of character and good at dealing with people, so she took over staff management. Meg was in charge of office work so Annie could direct her own energies to her favourite sweet-making. She worked alongside Arthur Smee and together they spent hours devising new recipes.

One day she called for a family meeting after the factory was closed.

'It won't take long, honest. Arthur and I want to show you something.'

On cue, Arthur wheeled in a trolley piled with smart golden boxes, alongside sampling trays of rich-looking, velvety-smooth dark chocolates, each one decorated with a tiny crystallised fruit.

'Go on, taste. It's our new line.'

Aunt Bess popped one in her mouth.

'Delicious, a bitter orange filling. These'll be expensive.'

Annie watched reactions carefully as the samples swiftly vanished. Arthur produced another trayful.

'Steady on,' Uncle Albert said. 'No point eating all the profits.'

'They'll never sell round here. Much too expensive for our end of Castle-thorpe,' frowned pessimistic Jim.

'They're designed for the big city stores, Leeds, Manchester, even London one day. Just right for the Christmas season, too,' Annie explained to the others.

The family stared in amazement at this further proof of Annie's genius and wondered where it would all end. Meg found it all very exciting.

'What's it called?' she asked.

She picked up a box and read the

black embossed label.

'Harmony Gold. I love it.'

Vincent bit into a rum marzipan.

'This'll knock Hetherington's so-called quality stuff right off the top shelves.'

'That,' Annie said, handing round more samples, 'is the intention.'

On a bright autumn morning Jack Hetherington met his brother, William, for their customary gallop over the Dales. He needed to discuss a serious business problem with his brother, and he needed to put his new high-spirited hunter through his paces. The horse was skittish. Jack cracked his whip just a little too hard and the animal reared in protest, slewed round, threw his rider and galloped off full tilt in pursuit of his own freedom. Jack was fatally injured.

As Lady Marcia, his sister-in-law, told the editor of the Castlethorpe Echo, Jack Hetherington died as he would have wished, in the saddle.

'We are only thankful we have the

rest of the family to carry on Hetherington's fine traditions in the town,' she added.

She meant, of course, her side of the family and even as the funeral cortège processed from Hetherington Hall, she was plotting to make sure it was George who held the reins and, hopefully, Ted, when he got all this reporting nonsense out of his system.

Jack's boys were too young as yet to have much impact. It couldn't be working better in Marcia's favour. She planned her next move to coincide with the special board meeting called by George and the firm's accountant. But Lady Hetherington was in for a shock. After formal condolences for Jack's death, Cyril Jeffries, the accountant, produced a set of sales figures which made grim reading.

'How can this be?' Marcia frowned. 'You're showing a loss, Cyril.'

'With respect, Lady Hetherington, I am not showing a loss, Hetherington's is. Mr Jack was aware of the situation and he'd been worried for some time. He intended talking to Sir William the sad morning of his accident.'

'Yes, he did mention something,' William began.

His brother's death had hit him hard. He wasn't interested in sales figures any more, hadn't been for some time. Getting old, time to retire, let the young ones take over, he thought.

'George,' Marcia snapped, 'did you know?'

'Of course. What do you think this meeting's about?'

'You should have told me.'

'Ma, you're not officially a director. You attend when you feel like it, and when we allow it.'

'That must change, from now! With Jack gone, and William retiring soon, you need me on this board, with full voting powers.'

'We can't do that, Ma.'

'Yes, we can. We are a family business, not a public enterprise. We make the rules. William?'

'Whatever you want, dear. I confess I'm a little weary of it all. Anyone object to Lady Marcia's appointment to the board?'

Satisfied she was now an accredited power at Hetherington's, Lady Marcia wasted no time.

'George, I want to know why our sales have slipped so badly. For years our turn-over has been steady. We've a monopoly in this area and retailers have to buy from us.'

'I'm afraid you're wrong, Aunt Marcia,' Cedric Hetherington spoke up.

He wasn't Jack's son for nothing and sensed the beginning of a family battle. He knew when to bide his time and when to speak up.

'What would you know?' Marcia said crushingly.

'More than you apparently, Aunt. Apart from trade being depressed there's a lot of new competition.'

'George?'

Marcia deliberately moved the discussion back to her son.

'Cedric's right,' he answered. 'There's a new company in Bradford manufacturing boiled sweets, intended for the open markets but lots of sweet shops are buying them and it's given the Bradford firm a toe-hold. There's a chap doing van sales direct to retailers. Started with one van but now he's got four on the road.'

'But he has to buy wholesale from us.'

'No. You must have heard of the new business, been going over two years. I'm amazed you've not heard.'

'How could I? That's trade.'

George rolled his eyes heavenwards.

'If you're to be an active board member you must know about these things, and what's Hetherington's but trade. Great-grandfather started out from a back kitchen, didn't he?'

'That was then. Quite different.'

'You've got to face facts, Ma. We've been complacent. Uncle Jack's motto was ever watchful, take nothing for granted. We've failed on both counts and let Annie Fletcher's Northern Candy steal a march on us, and to be fair, I can't help wishing her luck. She's got guts, business flair and intelligence.'

George leaned back, pleased with himself. He'd vowed to work hard for Hetherington's now he had Caro and a family on the way to look after and if he didn't make a stand, Ma would be trampling all over them. Marcia was looking as pole-axed as a woman of elegance could be. The worm was turning and no mistake but she was a match for that. Then it clicked.

'Who? Northern what? Annie Fletcher? I've heard that name.'

'Yes, dear,' William said, 'she's that pretty girl at George's wedding ball. You weren't all that kind to her.'

'Kind!' George butted in. 'Downright rude, more like, and she's a good friend of Ted's, too.'

'Ted? My Ted? That Annie Fletcher, the little nobody he insisted on bringing? She's Northern Candy?'

'She is,' George replied.

'And a friend of my son's? How long?'

'Quite a long time, five years at least.'

'And no one saw fit to mention this to me?'

'Why should we? Ted's an adult and he did bring her to the ball. You chose to ignore her.'

'Well, now I do know, I want all the facts and figures about Northern Candy and about Annie Fletcher. Is she undercutting our prices?'

'No. They're quality products, and some are more expensive than ours. Annie's just launched a stunning new range of de-luxe chocs, Harmony Gold. Breaking all records with it, she is.'

'No need to sound so pleased, George. Whose side are you on?'

'Hetherington's, of course, but we have been slack. If it takes Annie to make us pull our socks up that can't be bad.'

'I'll soon stop her. We'll buy out her piffling Northern Candy.'

'It's not piffling,' Cyril said, in his dry

accountancy manner. 'I've seen the turnover for the past twelve months.'

'We shall soon put her in her place. As for her seeing Ted, I shall deal with that personally. Now, let's get to work.'

★　★　★

'Well done, Meg, this copy's a treat. You've a real flair for advertising slogans. You'll have to have an assistant soon.'

'Not bad, is it? I love working for Northern Candy. Annie, you're so clever to have done all this.'

'Christmas was a record. We just can't seem to go wrong.'

'Careful, Annie. Pride before a fall.'

It was Friday night and the sisters had worked late to be clear for the Bank Holiday weekend.

'Finished?'

Annie went to switch off the lights and lock the office.

'Almost.'

Still Meg hesitated, then in a rush

she said, 'Annie, can we talk about Tom? It's over six years now and if he doesn't come back . . . '

'Don't! I don't want to hear.'

'I must. You're wasting your life. What sort of future is there for you when you're living in a dream? On your own you've made Northern Candy what it is, a success. Can't you have a personal life as well? You can't go on waiting for a miracle to happen or you'll end up a miserable old maid.'

'Stop it, Meg. I don't want to quarrel with you. I'm more than happy building up the firm, and waiting. Can't you accept that?'

'No, I can't, and what about Ted? He thinks the world of you.'

'Ted's a friend, that's all, and he's hardly ever here. I haven't seen him for six weeks and two days.'

'Aha!'

Annie bit her lip. She'd marked the time in her head that morning. It wasn't meant to be spoken aloud.

'Oh, Meg, do drop it. There's

nothing more to be said. Let's just be thankful we're doing well. Mam's even finally persuaded Dad to put his name down for one of those new houses to be built on the hill.'

'My, my. It'll kill him, moving from Nightingale Street. I'll miss it, too.'

'No, you won't. You'll soon be moving out, and what about young Arnold in the office? Seems to me he's pretty sweet on you.'

'Now you stop it, Annie. Let's go home. Hey, why don't we call in at the fair tonight?'

'Don't think so. I've got things to do.'

But Meg persisted and to keep the peace, Annie agreed. She had to admit it was fun. She remembered fairs with Tom. The first time he'd kissed her had been at the fair, behind the fortune-teller's tent. He'd said to her, 'I know your fortune, Annie. It's with me, for always,' and he'd kissed her on the lips. She'd nearly died with excitement. Somehow that girl had nothing to do with Annie now. It was like looking at another person.

She put her hand to her mouth in shock.

'What is it? Annie? You've gone pale,' Meg exclaimed.

'Nothing. I was just thinking that's all.'

Another person! What if Tom, too, was another person? What if it was true what everyone said? For the first time she felt the chill of doubt.

'Meg, can we go now?' she said.

'Just a while longer. I want my fortune told. Look, Gypsy Rose Lee. Wait here. I must know.'

'No. Meg!'

Too late, however, as Meg rushed into the future leaving Annie agonising over the past, until her sister came out of the tent.

'Guess what, four children, a handsome husband, a thousand pounds a year, and a journey over the sea. I can't wait! Now your turn, Annie.'

'No, I don't want . . . '

But Meg pushed her through the tent

entrance and Gypsy Rose Lee had sternly indicated she should sit. Annie gave her silver and the dark woman began to drone on about wealth, health and happiness for those who wait. Suddenly she stopped, her voice changed and her eyes pierced to the heart of the crystal. She gasped and her voice changed to a strange, high pitch.

'There's a fair young man, tall and broad, but he's not where he belongs. It's sunny, the man squints into the sun, he's tanned, his eyes are blue, no grey. The man's got a burden . . . dark clouds . . . he tries to push away.'

'Is he happy?' Annie whispered.

There was a long silence before the woman spoke again, this time in her normal voice.

'I can't tell that. I can't see more, just a man in a land of light.'

The gypsy sat back, eyes closed. Annie left the tent quietly.

'Well?' Meg asked, impatient. 'You were an age, twice as long as me. What did she say?'

'Oh, nothing, the usual rubbish, eight children, two thousand a year and two handsome husbands. That's why I was twice as long,' she teased, trying to recover from the shock.

The fair man was Tom, no doubt of that, and he was alive somewhere, overseas. France? The land of light? But where? And how could she find him? That night she dreamed of Tom for the first time in a long time. He was trapped in a deep pit and the dream turned to a nightmare as the trapped man turned his face towards her. She screamed out loud and woke, shaking. It was dawn before she fell into a troubled sleep and for the first time ever she was late for work.

★　★　★

'George? May I come in?'

'What is it, Ma? I'm frightfully busy. I'm having to grovel to the confectionery buyer at Forsythes. If we lose them it will be a blow.'

'Lose Forsythes? How?'

'Northern Candy, I'm afraid. It's business, Ma. All's fair. They've got a cracking new salesman and a damn good range of products. We'll have to put on our thinking caps.'

'That's why I want to see you. I've talked to Cyril and he agrees with me to nip it in the bud. Buy out the girl or whoever's behind her.'

'There's no one behind Annie except her family. They're a grand team. She's building an empire for her fiancé to take on.'

'Her fiancé? That's a relief. She can't set her cap at Ted if she's already engaged. What's the fellow do?'

'Oh, he's dead, poor chap. Killed in France. Don't worry, Ma. I doubt you'd understand.'

'Dead or alive, buy the woman out, now, George. I mean it.'

'If you and Cyril say so I'll make the offer. But she won't take it.'

★   ★   ★

'Well, I'm quite bowled over, flattered, too,' Annie said, pouring George Hetherington a cup of tea. 'Hetherington's wanting to buy me out. Am I really such a threat?'

'We'll survive but a fight's costly, and I can make a reasonable offer.'

'You know my answer, of course, George. Waste of time trying, but thanks. Genuinely thank your board for their interest. Now, have you heard from Ted lately?'

'Not a whisper, but all his reports are in the newspapers. Doesn't sound too wonderful in Europe.'

'Do you think he's safe?'

'As houses. Have you heard?'

'He telephoned me here at the office last week. He's fine, he says.'

'I expect he is then. Thanks for the tea, Annie. I'll report your answer to the board, and don't say I said so but Harmony Gold's splendid. Caroline's favourite.'

'Good. Take her this box from me.'

'Thanks, Annie. I saw them stacked

up in the corner. Thought you'd never offer!' he teased, good-natured.

As Annie saw George off the premises she thought how nice he was, how easy it was to relax in his company, just like with Ted, not a bit like his snob of a mother.

A week later, at exactly the same hour, Lady Marcia Hetherington was shown into Annie's office.

Annie was cool politeness.

'Lady Hetherington, do sit down. Would you like some tea?'

'Thank you, no. You turned down my son's offer.'

'Hetherington's offer to buy Northern Candy? Yes, I did, but thank you.'

'I have come in person to increase that offer, a little, and to tell you I believe it would be in the best interests of your employees to accept.'

'I appreciate that and I appreciate you coming personally but Northern Candy is not for sale, not at any price.'

'I cannot believe that.'

'You must, and that's that, Lady Hetherington.'

'How dare you speak to me so? Don't you realise my position in Castlethorpe?'

'Of course I do, but here in my work premises, we are on an equal footing. Both sweet-makers, aren't we?'

'I am not a sweet-maker, I'm a director of a long-established company. You are nothing but a jumped-up girl. I demean myself, coming here out of kindness, out of . . .'

For once words really did fail Marcia Hetherington. She felt a terrifying, raging anger surge through her and her voice rose to a scream.

'You foolish girl! You'll regret this. I'll not buy you out. I'll put you out of business completely and then see where your precious family ends up, in the gutter where you all belong!'

'Lady Hetherington, I think you should leave now. And perhaps you're the one who'll regret this. Please go.'

'I am going, but you'll be sorry you

ever thought of sweet-making, and don't you dare entangle my son, Ted, in your schemes. He is nothing to do with you and your sort and I absolutely forbid you to see him again.'

Annie felt almost sad for the woman who was rapidly losing control.

'Please, Lady Marcia, don't say any more. You are being offensive. Your chauffeur's here, he'll take you home. Thank you again for coming personally. Northern Candy is not for sale, and I shall continue to see Ted if he wants to see me. We are friends, you see.'

Marcia's howl of outrage brought startled faces to the office block windows and there was little work done at Northern Candy for the rest of that exciting afternoon!

8

Annie's confidence and authority had grown with Northern Candy's success but she still had a lot to learn about people. She believed in the basic decency of mankind so found it hard to imagine the venom motivating Marcia Hetherington. She couldn't know that, to Marcia, Annie Fletcher was an upstart who'd dared to step out of her class, challenge the Hetherington Empire and, worse, aspire to her son's friendship.

It was Vincent who brought the first piece of bad news.

'Woodhead's have cancelled their Christmas order, for all their Northern Candy outlets.'

'Cancelled? But why?'

Annie was preoccupied with a batch of toffee which had inexplicably developed a rancid taste.

'Alternative supplier. Better price, the buyer said.'

'But so near Christmas! Who's the alternative supplier?'

'It's not hard to guess, and the buyer dropped a broad hint. It's Hetherington's.'

'Ah!' Annie sighed.

'The old-boy establishment. Herbert Woodhead and Sir William — same school, same golf and social club, I'll wager.'

Albert confirmed it that evening.

'Ay, Vincent's right. As soon as the word was out that Hetherington's was in trouble, the ranks closed. Now Hetherington's has woken up to Northern Candy they'll fight dirty and show no mercy. You'll not beat the class system, Annie.'

'See if I don't. Our products are first class for quality and price. That's the only class that matters.'

'That's the spirit,' Albert applauded, concealing his misgivings.

Next, the van sales man from

Manchester demanded a discount for increased business to match Hetherington's price. Annie agreed.

'Commercial suicide,' Vincent said.

'Pooh! Arthur and I have a grand new line under test. Hetherington's won't be able to touch it.'

'What is it?' Vincent queried.

'Top secret. Only Arthur, myself and a couple of production workers know about it. You'll see, the sales'll soon soar.'

'I hope so.'

Vincent wanted to quit Northern Candy and work full-time at the Picture House but he'd see the business through this little crisis. At this point Vincent couldn't have known the little crisis was only the beginning of a wave of disaster. Annie was so preoccupied with her new line she didn't notice her mother's growing exhaustion. Joan had loved the early days of Northern Candy, managing the small staff of hand-picked relations and friends, but as the business grew the net had to be cast wider and inevitably pulled in a few rotten fish.

It was near the end of a day shift when a young girl whose white face matched her overalls crashed into Annie's and Meg's office.

'Annie, quick, your mam's being slaughtered. It's that Mabel Slattery. Nowt but trouble since she came, proper rabble-rowser.'

She ran after Annie and Meg who'd sprinted ahead of her. Uproar engulfed them as they burst into the production room. Girls were pushing and shoving each other, a long table was overturned, machinery spewing sweets out on to the floor.

'Stop it!' Annie yelled, jumping on to a chair. 'Everyone of you! Meg, over there, Mam's on the floor. Get that girl away.'

She jumped down, pushed her way to the end of the room where a hefty redhead was screeching abuse, punctuating it by banging Joan's head against the wall.

'Stuck up witch! Sack me, would you? You've had it in for me ever since I came here. Think you're somebody now you're a boss! Don't you forget, you still live in Nightingale Street, not Hetherington Hall just yet. You can't lord it over me. Take your rotten job and see if I care.'

Meg and Annie grabbed one arm each and pulled her away.

'Meg, call the police. Now you stop it you little vixen — ow!'

She let go as Mabel's teeth sank into her arm. The redhead stood back, panting, then delivered a vicious kick to Joan's ribs.

'You call the police and I'll burn this place down, see if I don't.'

She tore off her cap and overalls and tossed them on to the ground.

'Who's coming with me?' she challenged.

'Just go,' Annie shouted, on her knees beside her mother. 'Get off the premises and take your mates with you.'

A couple of girls, heads thrust back

in defiance, threw off their overalls and stamped off after Mabel whose parting shot was full of hatred.

'You'll be sorry, the whole blasted lot of you.'

Once Mabel and her gang had gone, the room was quickly put to rights, and Joan attended to. The rest of the women sheepishly returned to work. Joan was another matter. Sore and bruised physically, she was badly shaken mentally. It would take her weeks to recover her confidence. Jim forbade her to return to Northern Candy and for once Joan was glad of the firm male hand of her husband.

After the fight, several of the more timid girls left and rumours began rippling round the factory, that sales had plummeted, wages were to be cut, and the Fletcher family was riven with discord. All this was without foundation but morale slipped to a first-time low and the general atmosphere of Northern Candy was edgy.

Annie put her faith in the new line, a

wonderful confection of chocolate-covered fudge and toffee generously studded with raisins, nuts and cherries. This would lift everyone's spirits and set the firm back on the success trail. Vincent planned a big publicity launch for just before Christmas.

Annie worked like a demon but she had never forgotten the gypsy's vision. Somehow she had to find Tom, but going abroad was daunting. She'd never been outside Yorkshire in her life. Her hope was Ted. He'd written saying he'd be home for Christmas and looked forward to seeing her. Ted knew foreign parts and he'd surely help her.

A week before Vincent's campaign to put the new line in every Northern sweet shop, Arthur Smee burst into Annie's office.

'Damn and blast it, they've done it again. How on earth . . . '

Annie was shocked by her normally mild-mannered sweetmaker's show of temper.

'Sorry, but I'm that mad. I can't think . . . '

'What is it? Simmer down and tell me. Meg,' she called through to the adjoining office, 'can you put the kettle on? Arthur's in a bit of a state.'

'I'm not surprised, and the kettle's already on. Reckon we'll all need summat stronger than tea. How did it happen, Arthur?'

'God knows.'

He slumped into a chair, head in hands.

'We were that careful to keep it secret. Someone must have blabbed.'

Annie tapped her foot in frustration.

'What is the matter?'

'This.'

Meg had appeared and threw down the local paper.

'Hetherington's have a front-page spread and lots more inside. They're expanding premises, taking on more staff.'

'That's all right, we can match that with the new Sunburst launch.'

'Too late.'

Arthur flipped the pages.

'See, Hetherington's star product, a chocolate coconut fudge bar, and they've called it Starlight.'

Annie grabbed the paper.

'No one knew about our new line.'

'Someone did! It's no coincidence,' Meg said. 'It's quite deliberate, the timing, too, just before our own launch.'

'And it's already in the shops,' Arthur groaned. 'I passed Woodhead's and there's a big window display of Hetherington confectionery with Starlight bang in the centre. We're done for.'

'Don't be daft. It's only one line. I'll think of something. It's not the end of the world. Cancel the launch for a start then maybe we'll just gradually introduce Sunburst on to the market. Ours is a champion product and it'll speak for itself. Our main problem is much more serious. Someone at Northern Candy is passing on our secrets to Hetherington's and we've got to find out who otherwise it's going to happen again.'

It was a relief when Ted called at the factory one crisp sunny morning a week before Christmas with an invitation to drive Annie to their favourite walk by the river. The ground was hard beneath their feet as Ted tucked Annie's arm in his. They walked in silence.

'I think you're thinner. Hard work?' Annie asked, glancing up at Ted.

'Yes, but absorbing, like yours. I bet you haven't left that blessed factory in months, not since the last time I was home. How is it?'

Annie shrugged. For once she didn't want to talk about Northern Candy. There was something more pressing.

'I expect Christmas at the Hall will fatten you up.'

'Annie, I want you to come to the Hall on Boxing Day. There's a dance.'

'Be sensible, Ted. How can I come to Hetherington Hall?'

'George'll be there, Caroline, and the baby.'

Annie gave an unladylike snort of derision and resisted the temptation to tell Ted about Marcia's visit to the factory.

'Thanks, but no thank you. It's best if we stay in our own worlds.'

'You're very stubborn. I want you to be there.'

'Once bitten, twice shy. I'll not risk it. One day, when Northern Candy's bought out Hetherington's, I might condescend to visit.'

'You're not being fair.'

'Come on, it was just a joke. Let's forget about Northern Candy. I want to ask you something, a favour, to a friend.'

The cold had brought a rosy flush to her skin. Soft lips parted, brown eyes full of hope looked directly into his. It was how he'd pictured her so often when he was away. It was the most natural thing to kiss her. Beneath his lips Annie sighed as her body yielded to his. Why did it always feel so right when Ted held her? She put out her arms to hold him, remembered, and broke away. Ted pulled her back.

'What is it, Annie?'

'I'm sorry.'

'For what? Because I kissed you. Annie, admit it, you wanted me to.'

'Stop it, stop it, don't say any more.' She should never have come out with him. It wasn't fair. But they were only friends. Hadn't that been established? And she needed his help. But was it fair to ask him to help her find Tom? Her heart thumped, her brain whirled in confusion. Ted had stepped back.

'What's your problem, Annie?'

'I need to tell you something.'

'All right. We'll go back to the car. I've a flask of hot tea. It'll warm you.'

'I'm not cold, but tea would be nice.'

They turned back towards the car, walking apart. In the car, he tucked a rug round her knees, poured tea, and waited. Annie found it hard to begin.

'Well?' Ted prompted her.

'It's about Tom.'

Her hands curled tightly round the hot mug.

'Tom? Your Tom? Ormeroyd?'

'Yes.'

'You've heard something?'

The words tumbled out as she told him of the gypsy's vision, gathering conviction as she described the man with a burden in the land of light.

'I know it's Tom, it must be. I have to find him and I want you to help me, Ted. I don't know where to start.'

'You're fooling yourself, Annie. Your subconscious conjured up that apparition, your heart, not your head.'

'No, it's the truth. Tom's alive. I feel it. I always have.'

'How could he be? You can't believe Tom Ormeroyd is living somewhere in France, all this time, over seven years, never bothering to contact you.'

'But he can't. He's probably lost his memory, shell-shocked. I've read about such cases. He needs me to find him, to help him back.'

Ted took her empty cup.

'You're living in a dream world. It's time you grew up. Are you going to spend all your life chasing a childhood fantasy? I thought better of you, Annie Fletcher. I thought you had more courage, courage to face the fact that Tom Ormeroyd is dead. Do you hear?'

Annie gasped. Now Ted's eyes blazed anger, not passion. She recoiled.

'He's not dead. Why can't you face the truth? It's because you're jealous, jealous of Tom because I love him.'

'How can I be jealous of a dead man?' Ted exclaimed. 'Do you love him, Annie, really? Do you know this man, Tom, any more? You're carrying a dream in your heart, a dream lover, and you're scared of reality. That's why you work so hard, burying yourself in your factory, pretending it's all for Tom, but it's not, and that's a delusion, too. It's not for him any more, it's for you. You enjoy being Miss Northern Candy, being the boss, running the whole show. You'd no more want to share it with poor Tom Ormeroyd than turn it over to Hetherington's. You can't go back, Annie. It's too late. You're too fond of your confectionery empire, your new lines, your sales figures.'

'What do you know about our new lines?' she interrupted sharply.

Suddenly he was a stranger, someone from the other side, the enemy.

'New line? I only know what you told me last time I was home.'

'It's you! You told your mother about Sunburst, and everything else I told you. Taking me out to dinner, walks by the river, letting me prattle on about my ideas and plans!'

Frustration, exhaustion and disappointment overwhelmed her as she shouted accusations, hearing her voice become shrill, hating herself, unable to stop, seeing Ted's astonished face through a haze of hysteria.

'Stop or I'll have to slap you. I don't want to do that, so stop!' Ted said sharply and put his hands on her shoulders and shook her hard.

She jerked her head back then fell

against his shoulder and was quiet. Finally she gave a deep sigh. He released her.

'I'll take you back now. I'm sorry, I shouldn't have spoken of Tom like that. You're entitled to your dream. I have no business to take it from you.'

'I shouldn't have yelled like that. I don't know what possessed me.'

'You know it's nonsense, about me being a spy of some sort. I have no interest in Hetherington's as a business, only in my family's welfare. I think your grasp of reality is slipping. You need a break from work and . . .'

He stopped. There was no point talking about her obsession with a long-dead soldier. Time hadn't healed, it had done just the opposite. There was no hope and it was pointless trying to shatter her dream. She had to find her own way. It was time to let her be. At the factory gate, he handed her out of the car and kept her hand in his.

'A pity about today. The magic turned sour.'

146

'Oh, Ted. We both said things . . . '

He laid his hand on her lips.

'Don't say anything more, Annie. Just let's leave it there.'

He kissed her briefly on the cheek.

'I'll not forget you, Annie Fletcher.'

One last look into her soft brown eyes, then abruptly he was in the car and gone. Annie lifted her hand to wave but he didn't look back. As the car turned the corner she pressed her hand to her heart to stop the dull ache which she feared could well take up permanent residence.

9

The letter was amongst the Christmas post and Annie had a premonition of what it would say. Ted had left Castlethorpe to sail for America where he'd been offered a permanent job on a famous New York journal. It was a golden opportunity, he wrote, to start afresh and make use of the life he'd been spared in the war. His closing words had a dreadful finality.

I shan't forget you, Annie, but I know you are lost to me. Be happy with Northern Candy and be proud of what you've achieved.

It cast a shadow over Annie's Christmas which the family spent at Nightingale Street. The factory was closed for Christmas week and time hung heavily. It was Meg who decided enough was enough and she announced her plan over breakfast.

'This holiday's been a misery but as we've one more day, I've planned a treat — a day out in Scarborough. No arguments! Our Vincent's going to drive us in his grand new motor and we're going to enjoy ourselves. We're having a fish-and-chip tea in Whitby, so get your warm things on. Let's go.'

The family outing was a great success. For once the sun shone, pale wintry gold, but a stiff sea breeze put colour in their faces. Joan declared she felt a different woman at the end of the day and Annie and Vincent had a wonderful joint brainwave. Trade in the town was slow but there were a few day-trippers lured out by the sun and some shops were open.

At the Scarborough Rock Emporium, Annie and Vincent stopped dead.

'We could do that — seaside rock and novelties. What a grand new idea for Northern Candy.'

So, from that Fletcher day out, a new section of Northern Candy developed, and once more Annie was plunged into something absorbing and challenging. It was wonderful to be busy again. Annie worked hard with Arthur and his new assistant whose speciality was making rock and seaside novelties. Soon the stockrooms were ready for the seasonal trade, and sales figures began at last to inch slowly upwards.

It wasn't all plain sailing, though. Northern Candy was losing a steady trickle of local customers and every time there was a connection established with Hetherington's. Vincent also reported back that a Hetherington sales agent had been snooping around the seaside shops, too.

'They know every plan we have,' Annie said tartly, 'but it's a comedown for them, seaside novelties. Vincent, I've been thinking. I should travel more. Will you ... I'd like to go to France.'

'France! What for? You won't find any business in France.'

'I'm not thinking of sweets. It's Tom,' Annie replied.

Vincent rocked back on his heels. Nobody had spoken of Tom Ormeroyd for at least twelve months and he thought Annie was over all that nonsense about Tom still being alive. He'd actually seen Tom, just before he'd disappeared, though he'd never spoken of it. He'd seen him dive for cover into a shell hole and then seen that shell hole explode to the heavens seconds later. Nobody could've survived that. In the early days there'd been a chance he may have been wrong, but not now.

'I . . . I'm sure . . . '

She faltered. One look at Vincent's face told her it was useless. He would never believe her, he was too practical and down-to-earth to accept for one moment the gypsy's vision.

'It's nothing,' she said hastily. 'Forget it.'

He looked shaken. He thought he'd succeeded in erasing the memory of that flying debris, the carnage he'd witnessed in France.

'Nothing would ever drag me across the Channel to France. Nothing.'

'All right. Brighton, Bournemouth and London then.'

Strangely enough, Annie found herself obliged to go to London much sooner than she'd planned. A few weeks after her conversation with Vincent, an official-looking letter arrived addressed to the Director of Northern Candy, Castlethorpe.

'I'm not the the Director,' she said to Meg. 'I just make the sweets.'

'You made it happen. Open it.'

'I don't believe this. Look, Northern Candy's won an award. A prize for the best and most innovative new confectionery company in Britain!'

'In Britain! You're joking.'

'I'm not, read it. It's from the British Confectionery Association and they want us to go to London to receive a . . .'

Meg snatched the letter.

'A plaque and a cheque. A cheque, Annie! What shall we wear? London!'

She threw her arms round a bewildered Annie.

'You're so clever, our Annie, the cleverest woman in the whole of Yorkshire. Nay, in Britain! That's what it says.'

Annie was, for once, speechless, but Meg prattled on!

'All that publicity in the local paper, and those two men, remember, a few weeks ago? We thought they were factory inspectors. And now we're going to London! It's at somewhere called The Dorchester. Is that posh, Annie? We'll have to have new frocks.'

'Hold on, I can't go to London. If this is right, I'll send Arthur, or Vincent.'

'You will not! If you do I'll never set foot in this place again! See here, it says how many tickets do you wish to reserve? You're free plus one, and then there's me, Mam, Dad, Vincent, Uncle Albert, Auntie Bess, Arthur.'

Annie sat down with a bump.

'Well, our Meg, you don't give me a

lot of choice, and it will be champion publicity for Northern Candy.'

Vincent was to set the local publicity ball rolling right away and the women would have to go to Leeds for suitable outfits. It would all cost a fortune but they'd worked like demons and deserved a treat. And he had an old pal in London with newspaper connections! National publicity for Northern Candy wouldn't come amiss!

Once they'd left Castlethorpe Annie was sucked into the excitement and bustle of the big city and the grand occasion. She would never forget the moment she had to step out in front of the smartly-dressed company to receive her award. The Press had a field day. There were few women in industry in Britain in the 1920s, but none made the impact Annie Fletcher made that night in the Dorchester Hotel in London.

Two weeks later, Ted Hetherington, in a Chicago hotel, flicked idly through a trade magazine and exclaimed aloud as he recognised the smiling face beaming at him from the pages.

'My God, it's Annie!' he exclaimed.

Ted read the text about Northern Candy's achievements but it was Annie's face that riveted his attention. She looked so assured, so glamorous, and yet the young girl he'd first crashed into by the bank was still there, uncertain of her future, that question mark forever hanging over her.

'That's it, the question mark. I should have seen it before. What a fool I've been,' he said aloud.

At that moment, three thousand miles away, his mother was looking at the same photograph, practically choking over her breakfast with fury.

'Upstart creature. How on earth did she manage that?'

'What?'

Sir William was scanning the obituaries, a favourite occupation.

'That wretched girl. Look, that Northern Candy woman. Unless that girl is stopped we shall soon be bankrupt. I'm going to phone George.'

George was unhelpful.

'Good for Annie. Good for Yorkshire. Hetherington's will probably benefit by association.'

'But something has to be done,' Marcia insisted.

'Can't think what. Must dash or I'll be late at the office.'

'Men!' Marcia exploded into the dead phone set.

Crossing to her desk, she unlocked a concealed drawer, took out a notebook, and went back to the phone. The situation called for action.

It was Vincent, in the flat above the offices, who answered the thunderous banging and bell jangling just after dawn.

'What's up?'

His alarm at the sight of police uniforms jolted him wide awake.

'Sorry, Vincent, it's your factory. Fire. Started in the early hours I'd say.'

'No one's hurt? Annie wasn't there, was she?' Vincent said in horror.

He knew Annie often worked very

late with Arthur Smee.

'No, no. Someone's been round to your house in Nightingale Street. Annie was staying over. She's at the fire now with your dad and sister.'

'I'll get there right away. How bad?'

'The fire brigade's been there an hour or two. It'd well caught by the time they got there.'

Hours later, the work force stood in subdued groups amongst the skeleton remains of the factory. The Fletchers and Ormeroyds stood a little apart from the rest. Albert had managed to salvage piles of ledgers and records but everything else was lost. Annie stared in disbelief at the ruins of her years of effort, all vanished in a few hours.

'What was it all for?' she cried.

Vincent put his arm round her.

'Nay, Annie, it's a shame but don't fret. We're covered by insurance, no one's hurt, and all we need to rebuild is in your head, yours and Arthurs. That skill's not been lost.'

'I suppose,' she sighed, 'but to start all over again, from scratch!'

'Look at it this way,' Albert spoke up, 'we were planning on a move, what with the seaside rock expansion. This'll just push us along a bit faster. We can build a brand-new, up-to-date modern factory, with a bit of help from the bank, plus the insurance money.'

'We'd best be getting back,' Jim said. 'Nowt to do here.'

'I'll stay and talk to the girls. They'll be worried about their wages. Come with me, Meg,' Annie said.

A police officer interrupted Annie.

'Miss Fletcher? You're in charge of these premises?'

'Yes, or I was. Not much left to be in charge of now.'

'Just so, miss, but it's looking a bit serious now.'

'Serious? I should think it is. Six years of our lives gone up in smoke.'

'You misunderstand, Miss Fletcher. I'm afraid the fire wasn't accidental.

There's clear evidence it was started deliberately.'

Annie paled and Albert came closer.

'Just a minute, you're not accusing Annie or any of us of setting fire to our own business?'

'Not necessarily, though it's not unknown.'

'The officer means for the insurance money,' Vincent said angrily. 'That's ridiculous! Northern Candy's flourishing.'

'Now, sir, I didn't suggest for one second you were involved but we do have evidence of a person or persons involved.'

'Who?'

'We can't say at the moment but we'll let you know soon. In the meantime, I'd like you to be available, to ask you some questions.'

Annie bent her head. She mustn't let them see how close she was to tears. What hurt her more was that someone would deliberately set out to ruin her. But whoever it was they weren't going to beat her.

'Right, let's start looking for temporary premises. We'll get the staff to help. That way we can keep on paying them,' she said strongly.

It restored Annie's faith in human nature that Northern Candy was up and running in no time, albeit a very skeleton production line in very temporary premises. Everyone had worked all hours. The police officer investigating the fire came to see Annie in her tiny, temporary office.

'Bad news,' he announced grimly as he removed his hat and sat down. 'Arson it was, I'm afraid, without a doubt, and that may make a difference to your insurance claim.'

'But nobody from Northern Candy was to blame.'

'I'm afraid it was one of your ex-employees, a Raymond Bell. He kindly dropped his pocket book outside a window, footprints, too.'

'Raymond Bell! I can't believe it. Has he admitted it?'

'He hasn't denied it. He spoke very harshly of you.'

'I had to sack him. He was over familiar.'

'Ah! That explains a lot. Strictly off the record, Miss Fletcher, I should warn you there's evidence of a conspiracy to put Northern Candy out of business. We found a young woman called Slattery at Mr Bell's lodgings. Quite a character!'

'We did have an incident,' Annie interrupted.

'Quite. The Slattery girl was very forthcoming. Seems she'd had an argument with Bell over failure to pay her and her friends for disruptive actions in your factory.'

'So it was ultimately Raymond Bell responsible for leaking our secrets, and the fire. It's awful. I had no idea.'

'Mr Bell's a nasty piece of work, but he hints there's a bigger fish. I doubt he'll tell us, and he may be paid to keep quiet. Do you want us to investigate?'

'Yes. No! I don't want any more

trouble. I just want it to stop.'

'We could help.'

'No, I think I can handle this. I'd prefer it.'

'We'll be pleased to help in any way.'

He stood up and held out his hand.

'Good luck, Miss Fletcher, you've done a fine job here. Lots of jobs round here depend on you. Don't give up.'

'Don't worry. I shan't!'

Next morning Annie took a cab to Hetherington Hall. A man she took to be the butler told her Lady Hetherington never saw anyone at such an hour.

'I'll come in and wait. Tell her it's Annie Fletcher.'

'I'll see. You can wait in the study.'

Brusquely he indicated a closed door.

'Right. And don't be long or I'll be up there myself.'

It was twenty minutes before an immaculately-dressed Marcia came into the study.

'You have no right to come here at

this hour and demand to see me.'

'Lady Marcia, you must know why I've come.'

'What do you mean? How dare you!'

'You have been trying to destroy Northern Candy ever since I refused to sell to Hetherington's. I know you've been running a campaign to that end. I hope neither your husband nor son is involved. I cannot believe George would be a party to arson, nor Sir William.'

'Arson! What on earth are you talking about?'

'You don't know? You don't read the local newspaper? You didn't see Northern Candy's blackened remains?'

'Of course I saw, but what's that to do with me?'

'The police know Raymond Bell started it. And he hints there's someone, a bigger fish, behind him, instructing him, possibly paying him.'

'No, I never paid him.'

She stopped abruptly, the colour draining from her face.

'So, it is true,' Annie said triumphantly.

'No, of course not. Why would I want to know a man like this Bell?'

'Oh, I'm sure you have your finger on the pulse of lots that goes on in Castlethorpe. I found out Raymond Bell went to work at Hetherington's for a while, then he left, but he was there long enough to make his feelings about Northern Candy known. It's obvious it didn't take you long to pick that up.'

'You've no proof of any of this.'

'I'm sure Raymond Bell will tell the police everything. It could affect his sentence, I imagine.'

Annie crossed her fingers behind her back. She'd no idea if that was possible, but then, neither did Lady Marcia.

'He wouldn't. We had an arrangement. There is no way my name can come into this.'

'Well, I'll just have to let the police investigate further. I told them I'd handle it but if you . . . '

'You didn't give my name?'

Now sheer terror shone from Lady Marcia's eyes.

'I never meant him to burn the place down,' she shouted. 'Just stockrooms . . . do a little damage . . . not the whole building.'

'A bit difficult. Once a fire starts it doesn't pick and choose! Someone could easily have been killed.'

'I just wanted to stop you. The men, they wouldn't do anything. It just got out of hand, and Raymond Bell, he was the one. He played on my obsession. He hated you.'

'I know, now. I misjudged him, never believed he could be so . . . '

'So vindictive,' Marcia said bitterly. 'You've a lot to learn. What do you intend to do?'

'I don't want to hurt you, or your family. Your son is a good friend of mine,' she said calmly, 'and whether or not Raymond Bell tells the truth is up to him. All I want is for you to leave Northern Candy alone. If you don't promise, or if you break that promise, I swear I shall take legal action against you personally, and Hetherington's, too. You may employ clever lawyers to defend you but you'd never live down the publicity of truth.'

Lady Marcia was silent, torn between a strong desire to have the girl thrown out, and a streak of commonsense that told her she was beaten and had better make the best of it. In spite of herself, she felt a grudging admiration for the girl's courage and determination.

'Very well. I agree.'

'No more actions against Northern Candy? No more infiltration of spies?'

'Henceforth, I shall have nothing whatsoever to do with your company.'

'Good. I won't need your written assurance. I trust your word.'

Marcia was beaten but resilient, and was rapidly regaining poise and dignity. She hesitated, then forced out the words, 'And I hope all goes well in rebuilding your business. I never meant it to go this far.'

'Thank you, Lady Hetherington.'

As the Hall door closed behind her, Annie executed a little jig of triumph on the broad marble stairs. It had worked! The confrontation had come off. She was sure there'd be no further trouble from Hetherington's. She practically skipped down the wide drive, her head racing with plans for the future — the new factory, starting all over again. It was a challenge she relished. From now on she would concentrate on making Northern Candy the finest sweet factory in Britain. She couldn't wait to get back to the office.

Absorbed in dreams of the future, she didn't hear the motor until it swept round the corner, hooting furiously to warn her out of its path. She stepped aside but the car screeched to a halt a few yards ahead of her. Her heart leaped as the tall, familiar figure jumped out.

'Annie! Whatever are you doing here?'

'Ted! What are you doing here? Why aren't you in America?'

'I've come home, to see you.'

He took her hands in his, resisting the impulse to pull her into his arms.

'I need to talk to you, Annie. Why are you at Hetherington Hall?'

'I was visiting your mother. Ted, I can't stop now. There's so much to do. There was a fire, Northern Candy was destroyed, but we'll start afresh.'

'A fire? Annie, we have to talk. Meet me tonight. There's something important I have to tell you, about Tom. I think I may have traced him. There's a strong possibility that Tom is alive and you've been right all these years.'

10

That evening, in a small hotel in the Dales, Ted ordered dinner for both of them. Annie was incapable of making any choices that night. He pushed her glass nearer.

'Drink some wine. You look too pale. It's been a shock,' Ted said. 'By the way, congratulations on your award, Annie. It was your picture in a magazine which brought me back here.'

'Really? I'm glad. I've missed you. You're a good friend,' she said hurriedly, trying to shut off the memory of her heart's joyful leap when she'd seen him in the Hall driveway.

'And the fire? George told me about it.'

'Terrible at first, but Uncle Albert's going to retire from the bank and . . . wait, I shouldn't even be thinking about a new factory. You've actually found Tom?'

'We think so, but I can't be absolutely sure.'

He hesitated, checking that his own emotions were well under control. If it was Tom Ormeroyd they'd found deep in the heart of rural Burgundy, then this was the last service he could render Annie. He spoke evenly as he told her his story.

'You looked so happy in the picture at the awards ceremony, but I know that's not truly possible because of your conviction that Tom is alive. When I left England I thought I could forget you and your dream. I was wrong. I couldn't forget, so I set out on this impossible mission, to find one of the thousands of missing believed killed from the war. I checked records in London, then went to France to meet an old friend who's writing a book about the missing men of war. He'd established an enormous network of contacts and he set the Tom Ormeroyd ball rolling for me. We traced a Thomas Oomerod, working in a vineyard in Vevers, a village in Burgundy.'

Annie found that hard to imagine. Tom was dynamic, full of restless energy. She associated vineyards with a sleepy, rural life, not the setting for the Tom she remembered.

'Apparently, but you must be prepared for disappointment. It may not be your Tom. The spelling of the surname is slightly different. We have to go to Vevers to identify him. You may find it hard to accept what you find there.'

'Why? If it is Tom, we just pick up the threads where we left off.'

'Do you honestly believe that? Can't you see how different things are, how changed you are? You're a successful businesswoman, head of a flourishing company. How will Tom fit in?'

'He will. Can't you understand? I did it all for him. He'll love it.'

'We'll see,' Ted said. 'I've booked the steamer from Dover, tomorrow.'

'Tomorrow! What'll I tell Mam and Vincent?'

'You'll think of something, a resourceful woman like you. Now, let's enjoy the rest of our evening. Tell me all about Northern Candy.'

It was the flimsiest of excuses but everyone swallowed it. Annie told them she was off on a fact-finding trip, to a model sweet factory outside Paris. Ted had contacts there and could introduce her to the owners.

As soon as they left Castlethorpe, Annie was gripped by the excitement of the journey. On board the steamship bound for Calais, she stood on deck with Ted and watched the white cliffs slip away. Ted enjoyed her eager pleasure and watched her bright eyes alight and eager not to miss a thing. And Annie loved every second of being abroad.

Paris enchanted her but after a brief whirlwind tour of the city, Ted hired a car and pushed south towards Burgundy. Neither could admit it but neither wanted the journey to end. Its outcome was uncertain but both knew it would change their lives for ever. On the outskirts of a pretty, little village, Ted stopped at a small inn.

'We'll stay here tonight. We're not far away from Vevers.'

'Shouldn't we go now? It's still daylight for a while yet.'

'I think you should rest, and it's so peaceful here.'

Annie climbed out of the car, stretched, and followed Ted to a seat in a small orchard. Her face upturned to the afternoon sun, she relaxed, while Ted arranged their accommodation. Tomorrow she'd see Tom.

Ted touched her arm and sat beside her.

'The ladies are busy now concocting the most delicious dinner the inn can offer. No one else is staying here so we can have their full attention. That's Yvette, signalling your room is ready. Dinner in two hours, out here.'

Indoors, Annie sank deep into the

feather mattress and closed her eyes. Small sounds outside the open window lulled her to sleep until she woke to a clatter of pans and wonderful aromas. She bathed her face, changed into a deep blue silk dress and went into the garden. A table was set under an ancient tree. Ted greeted her.

'You look rested,' he said but his eyes said so much more as he held out her chair. 'I hope you're hungry. Madame has cooked a banquet.'

'I'll manage, especially if it tastes as good as it smells.'

Annie never forgot that night. Ted produced champagne and madame and daughter, Yvette, darted and swooped around them serving course after delicious course. Yvette finally brought out coffee and sweetmeats before the two women left the twilit garden to Ted and Annie. Annie sighed.

'Thank you for bringing me here and for everything, Ted.'

'I hope you find what you want tomorrow, and if this Thomas Oomerod is your Tom, I promise to leave you.'

'No!' Her cry of dismay was involuntary.

'Don't worry, I'll see you back to England, if you want me to.'

'That's not what I meant. I . . . I can't . . . '

She couldn't tell him the thought of him leaving her life was unbearable. She stood up in distress as he came to her. He held her shoulders.

'You can't give up now, Annie. It'll be difficult, but if you love Tom . . . '

The question hung in the air.

'Annie,' he murmured and swept her into his arms.

No force on earth could prevent their lips meeting as he gathered her closer, before he gently put her from him.

'We're friends, Annie, never forget that. Now, we'd best go in.'

In her bedroom under the eaves Annie undressed slowly, not daring to think of the morning and not daring to admit what her heart was telling her.

Next morning she was reluctant to

leave the safe haven of the inn and travel those few last miles up the road to the unknown. As the road slipped by, her nervousness increased and when they finally drove slowly through the village of Vevers itself she felt as though she might faint.

'Are you all right?' Ted asked.

'Yes. Where's the actual vineyard?'

'Not far. A mile or so, according to my directions.'

Annie clasped and unclasped her hands in tension. Ted pointed to a low stone wall beyond which orderly rows of green vines appeared to stretch to the horizon. He swung the car through a gap in the wall and pulled up by a row of outbuildings which ran parallel from a tall stone house.

'It's lovely,' Annie said quietly, 'but there's no one here.'

Ted pointed to a low doorway where an old man emerged, blinking in the sunlight, shading his eyes as he came towards them. Ted spoke to him. He replied, pointing to the fields.

'Everyone's working the vines, and, yes, there is an Englishman here.'

'Mais oui,' the man interrupted eagerly. 'Monsieur Thomas.'

He gestured towards the man. Annie took a step forward, looking and looking as the figure became clearer.

'Tom?'

Ted watched Annie's face intently as she watched the man.

'I don't know. He has such a beard, and he walks so badly . . . a limp.'

Then the man was upon them. He took off his hat and smiled. Annie's heart thumped rapidly. Those blue-grey eyes, startling against his tanned face — how could she have forgotten them.

'Yes,' she said, 'it's Tom. Tom Ormeroyd.'

The man looked puzzled, his welcome smile fading.

'You're English, and you know my name.'

'Tom,' Annie cried, 'it's me, Annie, from Castlethorpe. Yorkshire! Don't you know me?'

'I don't think so, but I am pleased to see you. We get very few visitors from England. Are you here to buy wine? We have some fine vintages. Why don't you come into the house and have a glass of our Burgundy?'

He began to walk towards the house.

'But, Tom, don't you remember? The war, and you never came . . . '

'Sh,' Ted whispered. 'Be careful. We don't know for sure yet.'

'I know it's our Tom!'

Annie was near to tears as Ted went on.

'You don't know his mental state. Go slowly, Annie. You could do damage. He does not, at this moment, remember you.'

The man, Tom, turned back and gave her a strange look, then beamed with relief as a pretty dark woman came running out of the farmhouse. She called out in French and Tom answered her fluently. She smiled and held out a hand to Annie.

'Welcome to our vineyard. Please

come in. My husband will bring one of our special bottles. We see few English people and I know my husband longs for the sound of a true English voice. Come, please.'

Her English was heavily accented. Ted put his hand under Annie's arm.

'Husband?' she whispered.

'Hush. Slowly remember. It's been seven and a half years — a lifetime!'

It was the strangest hour Annie had ever passed. The enormous kitchen was cool and dark, smelling of fruit and spices, and when Tom opened a bottle of rich red wine there was a glorious aroma. Tom looked at Ted as he tasted the wine and Annie looked at the girl called Marie, Tom's wife!

'This is excellent wine,' Ted said as he nodded approval.

'One of our best vintages.'

Tom offered Annie a glass. His expression as he looked at her was puzzled but his main attention was focused on Ted.

'You see, I'd like to ship some of this to England.'

He launched into a business plan for exporting his Burgundy.

'Thomas is ambitious,' Marie whispered to Annie. 'He has such plans.'

'Yes, I can believe that. How long has he been here?'

'Tom has been here since one year after that dreadful war. We found him wandering among the vines, in such a terrible state . . . his leg . . . you see how he limps, and he has bad headaches. He had many scars from wounds but we nursed him here and gradually he healed, and began to work with the vines. He learned so quickly.'

Marie rattled on, sometimes breaking into French. Annie was glad to sit and let Marie's voice wash over her. She'd imagined it would be Tom at the vineyard, or not. She hadn't bargained for a Tom whose past life seemed to have been totally erased with no memory of her whatsoever.

All these years she'd been living a

dream. She looked at Tom now, in deep discussion with Ted. He had a folder on the table, flipping through the contents. Plans for a wine empire, no doubt. The entrepreneurial streak lived on! But apart from that he was a stranger. She felt no leap of the heart, no excitement. In truth, he was a different person, just as she, Annie, had changed. With a terrible feeling of guilt she recognised she couldn't, didn't, love this bearded stranger. Perhaps she uttered a small sound of acknowledgement because Ted looked up and smiled. It was then Annie felt that excitement of the senses she was now free to recognise.

At that moment, the door burst open and a toddler staggered unevenly towards Tom.

'Papa, Papa,' he chanted, throwing himself at Tom's knees.

Tom picked him up and swung him around.

'And where is your nana? You've run away from her again.'

'Your son?' Annie asked unnecessarily.

'But of course,' he said, his voice full of pride. 'We'll have lots more little Thomases, Marie and I, to help build up our winery, a real family business.'

'And your family in England?'

In spite of Ted's warning look Annie had to ask the question. Tom looked directly at her, narrowing his eyes, then he looked to Marie to answer.

'We have no clues to Thomas's past life in England. All he had was a scrap of document and from that we made out his name, Thomas Oomerod. He remembers an explosion, and a year's wandering as a beggar, nothing else. But you knew him in England? You know of his family?'

'No, no, a mistake. Your husband is not the Tom Ormeroyd we thought,' Ted interrupted swiftly. 'Your son is a fine boy, and you have a happy life here in the sun.'

Marie had moved to Tom's side, holding his arm protectively.

'Yes, we do.'

Tom embraced his wife. To Annie he looked perfectly in keeping with wife and child in the old French farmhouse.

'You'll call again?' Tom asked politely.

'I'm sure we will,' Ted replied, taking Annie's arm. 'Some day soon.'

They drove a mile or two away from Vevers before Ted stopped the car.

'Let's walk for a while. There's a river beyond that field.'

They walked side by side for a while until Ted took Annie's hand and drew her closer to him.

'Annie, are you very upset?'

She stopped and turned to him.

'Why, no! Tom's happy, he has a lovely wife and son, and a business, and plans. He doesn't need me or Northern Candy. I've fooled myself for years that I was building Northern Candy for Tom. I was at first, but it was for me. I've been stupid. I'm sorry.'

There was no regret or sadness in her voice, just plain matter-of-factness.

Ted tucked her arm in his in the way

she loved and carried on walking.

'Shouldn't we help him recover his past, though, and what about Uncle Albert and Aunt Bess? We can't pretend he's dead now.'

'I think we should go back to England and get medical advice.'

'Would it be so bad for Tom to find his memories? Marie and his children could share them, too.'

'And what if he fell in love with you again?'

'Oh, Ted, that's foolish. Didn't you tell me endlessly how different I was from that young girl? Besides, I could never love Tom because I . . . '

She stopped, suddenly aware of total silence. They stood together as one until Ted spoke softly.

'Annie, if you don't love Tom I can say what I've held back for long years. I love you, Annie Fletcher, I love you truly and deeply. Will you marry me?'

Her heart was full of love for Ted. It had been there a long time and she'd been too selfish and blinkered to see it.

She was thankful Tom was happy and content with his life and maybe one day she could be a small, past memory in it. She stepped away from Ted.

'Marry you? That's impossible — a Hetherington and a common Fletcher? What would Lady Marcia say? She'd never survive the shock.'

For a second Ted's eyes registered disbelief, then he saw Annie's sparkling eyes, and he pulled her into his arms.

'Don't do that again, ever,' he said, smiling. 'You will marry me?'

'Of course I will. I've loved you for so long. I've been a fool. Let's not waste any more time because I can't bear to be without you, except . . . I have to keep Northern Candy. You realise that?'

'Annie Fletcher, you are Northern Candy and it'll always be an important part of your life. You're a modern woman and I love you for that.'

They kissed before Annie had the final word.

'But we'll have time for other things, too. Northern Candy's a family firm.

We'll need . . . '

As Ted put his lips to hers, his face told her he thoroughly understood and approved of all she'd dreamed of — a happy marriage, a man she adored, and a growing family!

THE END